twelve and a Half Hearts

IAN CAHILL

TWELVE AND A HALF HEARTS

Copyright © 2016 Ian Cahill

All rights reserved.

Published by Smile Your Head Off Press 2016

Kansas City, Missouri, United States

This is a work of fiction. Any similarity between the characters and situations within its pages and places or persons, living or dead, is unintentional and co-incidental.

Cover Design from paperandsage.com

For Cara, Harper, Sawyer,
Marty, and The Wordwraiths

Table of Contents

CHAPTER ONE
Mr. Potter 1998

It was all pageantry, as it should have been. It was a high school graduation, after all. I was lingering in the back of the auditorium. I wasn't a respected enough faculty member to be present up on the stage, not that I would have wanted to be.

I normally wouldn't bother coming to the graduation of my students. If I hadn't been personally asked to attend, I would have been sitting in a coffee shop working on my attempt at a novel, instead.

As the procession began, students shuffled into the auditorium wearing the traditional cap and gown. From the back, I had a ringside view of the class as they made their way to the seats in the middle of the giant room. I kept a watchful eye on every student that passed, waiting to see her.

I shifted in my sports jacket with a nervous feeling, patting the precious contents inside. As the students passed by, some of the guys shouted "Yo, Mr. Potter!" while the girls smiled and offered coy waves in my direction. It was nice, but my thoughts drifted to Sue.

***

Sue Anderson, that year's valedictorian, had stopped me in the hall one morning in early April to make sure I would be attending. She leaned against a bank of lockers and tucked a handful of folders behind her back. She asked me to come, plainly and nonchalantly. I wasn't too keen on the idea.

"You know I have a speech right?"

"Sue, of course I do. I'm pretty sure they always let valedictorians speak."

"So you're coming then?"

"Graduation isn't for another six weeks."

"I know, but I found out today that I'm a lock, so I am going to start working on my speech. Are you going to come or not?"

"Well I wasn't planning on it. It's not really my thing." I could tell she was disappointed.

"Oh." She pushed herself off of the lockers and tucked her curly blonde hair behind her ear. She looked me straight in the eyes and I noticed her lip quivering. Before she could say another word, Marjorie Simmons approached.

"Sue, don't forget we moved the meeting to Mrs. Satchel's room this afternoon," Marjorie said. Her shrill voice itched inside my ear.

"Yep, no worries. See you there."

Sue took a few steps towards Marjorie, who had already moved further down the hall and almost around the corner. When she disappeared, Sue spun around on her heels to face me.

"You know how hard it was for me to ask you to come?"

"I'm sorry?"

"Well, it was really hard. I asked myself, of all of my teachers, who would be the most proud, who would I most want to hear me speak." She looked at her feet. "It was you. It's always been you."

I was caught off guard. I didn't realize she felt so strongly about the invite. I should have realized she was being serious—she always wore her hair down when she was at her most attentive.

"Don't take it personally. I tend to avoid situations where there's a large number of faculty members all in one place."

"You mean, like every day at school?"

Dammit. I could do nothing but marvel at her in the moment. Whether it was her take on *A Doll's House* and its portrayal of woman's rights or her views on the burden of Gregor Samsa in Kafka's *Metamorphosis*, she always had just the right thing to say. She might as well have been my Dorian Gray.

"Okay, fine. You've backed me into a corner, clever girl. I'll come, but don't go telling the whole world. I'd hate for this to become a habit."

A smile materialized across her face, her cheeks flushed with red.

"Oh thank you Mr. Potter! Thank you, thank you!" She reached out and tapped my shoulder, "I gotta go, two papers and a test to ace. You just made my week Potter, you know that right?"

"Alright, knock it off, that'll just go to my head," I flashed her a grin and turned towards my classroom. I was going to graduation. If there was any student with the chutzpah to convince me to actually show up, it was Sue. She was without a doubt the most accomplished and bright student I ever had the pleasure of teaching.

I turned around just as I reached the end of the hall. Sue conducted herself with the utmost respect for those around her. I watched as she patted a friend on the shoulder, gave copy approval on an upcoming article for the school newspaper, and stopped to pick up a calculator that another student had dropped.

She certainly had an air about her and, whether I noticed it or not, she had pulled me into her good nature. I started to contemplate what I was going to wear to the graduation. I was in a sort of daze as I made my way back to my classroom. I weaved in and out of the crowd of students like a shark in a school of fish.

High school in the late nineties still clung to the idyllic images seen in the movies like *The Breakfast Club* or *Heathers*. All the kids at Taft fell into one stereotypical category or another. Unfortunately, there was a clear dividing line between the jocks and the academics. The exceptions to this rule were the soccer players.

The soccer teams for both the girls and the boys were some of the smarter kids at Taft. They managed to stay cool, not only with their peers, but also with their teachers. It was sort of like seeing a rhinoceros in the wild. You know they exist because you've seen them in pictures, but then you see one in real life and it changes your whole perspective.

Sue only played soccer during her sophomore year, but it was enough for her to be in the good graces of the team. She didn't have a falling out or quit due to poor performance. No, she simply weighed her already extraordinary list of activities, and soccer fell below the red line.

No one on the team could argue with Sue's well-reasoned decision to move on. It also didn't stop Sue from remaining friends with a majority of the girls on the soccer team. And since most were excellent students as well, they often shared AP classes together.

As it so happens, I taught advanced English to the senior class at Taft. This meant, of course, that I had the privilege of teaching Sue and her former soccer cohort, Ann and Rachel.

Rachel was from a family of athletic phenoms. Her Dad played soccer in the Olympics and her brother was in the NFL. But she was no slouch herself. She was heading to the All-American women's soccer team that year.

Ann was a little meek and not nearly as athletic. She wasn't dazzling anyone on the soccer field, but was good enough to make the varsity team. Her real talents lay elsewhere. Her passion was singing. She cut her teeth under the tutelage of an old family friend who went by the name of Siouxsie Sioux.

These three were a treat to have in class. Later that afternoon, the girls were discussing college acceptance letters. There was a pep rally assembly that morning for the boys basketball team which resulted in my lesson plan consisting of idle chatter.

For these three young women, it was pretty clear that each of their paths were about to head in different directions. It showed in the wide variety of colleges and universities each had applied to. It was sad, in a way, to think about these three inevitably splitting up. They knew it was going to happen, but rather than whine about it, they kept the conversation light.

"I got another call from the coach at UCLA. He practically offered to pay my tuition out of his own pocket to come play for him," Rachel cooed.

"Well, I had that dream again last night," Ann sighed under her breath.

"The one where you live out of your car and sing in all the famous bars from movies?" Sue inquired.

"Yep. This time I was singing at the coffee shop in *Friends*. I can never remember its name. My Dad would absolutely kill me if I ever did something like that."

"Just do it. That would be so much easier than choosing between the eight or nine schools my Dad insisted I apply to. I have a bunch of letters piled up at home. I can't bear to open any of them to see if I got in." Sue rolled her eyes and shook her head.

"Well, are they big envelopes or small ones?" Rachel asked.

"I don't know, big, I guess. I don't want to think about it, it gives me the chills."

I half listened to their conversation as I sat at my computer, savoring a Clark Bar and grading essays from the day before. The girls had pulled their desks into a triangle and rested their legs on each other elaborately, log-cabin style. I glanced back and forth between them and my computer.

"Sue, you know, I am a little offended you never asked me to write you a recommendation letter," I said, gently interrupting the conversation, "I'm pretty sure with my backing you would be a shoo-in at whichever school you chose from the pile."

Sue looked up, almost embarrassed as the other girls giggled, "You're probably right."

I could feel the heat from her smile.

Without speaking, I opened up the word processor on my computer and began drafting a letter. I figured I would give it to her the next day, a token of my appreciation. I stared at the blank white screen for a moment and then wrote the following:

To Whom It May Concern,

I am pleased to recommend Suzanne Anderson for acceptance to your prestigious University. For the past three years Sue has been a beacon of light in my classroom and those of my colleagues. I

7

have had the pleasure of getting to know her potential and ability. I have nothing but glowing compliments for her and her academics. She is an inspiration to the students around her and even more so to myself.

Sue has always put her studies first, and is nothing short of exceptional in all my classes. She is consistently in the top of the grading curve and is not one to shy away from class participation. This includes extracurricular activities. Sue has always been one to succeed and it shows in her work and interaction with her peers. She would lay down in traffic to help a struggling student. She cares about equality deeply and the success of those around her.

In my years as a teacher I can't think of a single student that has impressed me more, not only academically, but as an astonishing person in general. She is destined for great things and your university would be foolish to overlook her. I know I haven't.

Not a day goes by that I don't think of Sue and what she will become. Her personality and poise are second to none. She is remarkable in every way and I can't imagine a world that didn't include Ms. Anderson.

Sincerely,
Kevin Potter

Just as I had finished the first pass, the bell rang and the girls spent a few fleeting moments untangling their legs from each other. Sue stuffed her things back into her bag and gave me a half-hearted wave, coupled with a sheepish smile, as she slipped out into the hall.

By the end of the day I had almost forgotten about the letter, but made sure I emailed it to myself so I could proof it again that evening. It may have been a pointless reference letter, but since I had written it anyway, I had a responsibility as an English teacher to make it as flawless as possible.

When I arrived home, I tried to remember Sue's parents. I'd met them once at a National Honor Society dinner. How oppressive could they be? I couldn't imagine they were so overbearing that Sue felt the pressure to go to a college they picked. She was sharp in every way; she would have no trouble making it into any school she applied to.

I wondered if the letter would even matter, but reasoned the gesture stood on its own. I wrestled with the thought for over an hour before deciding she didn't need my letter. I climbed into bed that night still torn, but by the time I convinced myself to do it anyway, it was almost 2:30 a.m. and I couldn't keep my eyes open.

***

I pushed the memory out of my mind and continued to look through the crowd for signs of the only person in the room that cared if I came to the graduation.

The class of 1998 was one of the largest at William Howard Taft High and my hand was sore from all the high-fives students insisted on throwing my way. As the line waned, Sue had yet to materialize.

The processional music started to fade and I decided to move closer to the stage. I didn't want to hobknob with my colleagues, so I ducked into a breezeway. It was just dark enough to mask my presence. I was disappointed not to see Sue, but assumed she was somewhere practicing her big speech. From the breezeway, I had a clear view of the podium while still remaining in the shadows. I was free to make judgmental faces at the rubbish that would spew from the lips of my beloved Administrator.

I also had a decent view of the scores of parents sitting in the stands across from me, each excited about their son or daughter's passage into adulthood. As I scanned the crowd, all I could think about was how I wished I was off smoking weed under the bleachers somewhere. I was lamenting my lack of pot when I heard a voice.

"Mr. Potter?"

I turned to find the Valedictorian herself: Sue Anderson. I jumped into full-on teacher mode without even thinking. "Sue, what are you doing back here? Doesn't your speech start in a few minutes?" I cocked my head to the side and raised an eyebrow at her.

"I think I'm hyperventilating." She pressed the corner of her shoulder on the concrete wall next to her and let forth a bellowing sigh.

I rushed to her side just in time for her to collapse into my arms. She smelled of lilac and citrus and her commencement robes were silky smooth.

Sue whimpered and I pushed her shoulders towards the wall. "Are you all right?"

"I'll be fine. Probably just nerves."

I let out an exasperated huff. "Sue, weren't you on the debate team?"

"Well, yes! But this...this speech is going to affect the lives of everyone out there. It might factor into very important life decisions." Sue stood up at this point. I could see the momentum building.

I shuffled my feet for a moment, "Sure, some of them might cry today. But tonight, when they're getting wasted with their friends, they'll be thinking about sex, drugs, and the usual celebratory fodder. I think you give yourself a little too much credit, Sue. I mean, half those kids probably think you are a stuck-up bitch."

"Mr. Potter!" She punched me flat out in the arm. She was beginning to act more like the Sue I knew her to be. We exchanged a few laughs before she looked at her watch and began pacing.

"Why am I so nervous? You're right. I have my whole life ahead of me. I could literally vomit all over the stage and still manage to make my way through college and life in general."

"Then what you are so worked up about?"

"You weren't Valedictorian, were you, Kevin?"

I bit my lip a little at the sound of my name. I tried to come off as casual about it, but Sue must have realized how it sounded, and quickly corrected herself.

"Mr. Potter, all I mean is, it might not be a lasting memory for any of my friends out there, but this speech symbolizes all my hard work and determination in school. I mean, it's a reward of sorts. I don't want to let anyone down." She was once again breathing deeply. I started to move towards her to prevent another episode.

"Sue, listen to me. Rule number one of life: you will let people down. And it will be through no fault of your own. There will always be people around you that are clueless and can't recognize a good thing when they see it." With that, I did the only thing I could think of, short of placing my fists on my hips and posing like a superhero. I shrugged.

Sue looked me straight in the eyes. I couldn't tell if my eyes were watering or hers, but a haze enveloped her face. She jumped a little as an organ began playing in the distance.

We held our stare for a moment before she began to pace once more.

"Oh God, oh God..."

"Sue, aren't you going to walk with the processional?"

I must have said the wrong thing, because her doe eyes grew even wider. She started to tear out of the breezeway, then stopped. "It's too late, I'll look like an idiot if I go now! What do I do?"

"Sue, calm down. Your speech is near the beginning of the program, and you have an assigned seat in the front row. It's going to be fine." I grabbed her by the shoulders and looked her in the eyes. "I'll stay here with you until it's time, and you will, with confidence and dignity, stride towards the stage with your head held high. It'll be like Joan of Arc leading troops to battle or Karen in search of vodka on Will and Grace. You can do this." I punctuated the last sentence with a firm shake.

She looked up at me and smiled. "So what do we do while we wait?" she asked as she moved slightly closer to me.

I instantly let go of her shoulders and moved towards the opposite side of the breezeway. I adjusted my tie and touched the outside of my jacket, feeling the contents before checking my watch and then awkwardly smiling at Sue. "It shouldn't be too long. Did you decide on a university?"

She didn't answer, only twisted her toes against the concrete like she was putting out a cigarette or killing a June bug. I watched as she pulled out her speech and began murmuring to herself, like I was no longer there.

This went on for a minute or so, and then the auditorium got quiet. All the students had marched in and taken their seats. The head of the school board, Dr. Levi Braden, approached the podium and began his dull and ever-so-sarcastic keynote. His head barely made it over the top of the podium as he went on and on about the achievements of the class at large. He cited the girls' state swimming championship and the senior field trip to Washington, DC.

I had turned down an event program as I'd entered the building, but I was certain Sue had memorized it. She inched closer to the entrance as the Principal, Linda Stevenson, spoke. Linda went on about a dream she had, in which history books were filled with the achievements of the graduating class. It was far from convincing and I heard the uncomfortable shuffling of seats from the breezeway.

As Linda finished, I knew from Sue's body language it was time for her big speech. Linda was just beginning to rattle off the achievements of Sue Anderson, model student, when I felt her hot breath on my neck.

"Mr. Potter, thanks for talking me off the ledge. You were a great teacher and were always there for me. I'm really going to miss you."

I wasn't quite sure what to say as she peered up at me with doe eyes. I simply nodded, reached into my jacket and handed her my recommendation letter. I'd never gotten around to editing it, but I'd felt compelled to print it out and stuff it into an envelope on my way to the graduation.

Sue started to say something, but instead just took the envelope, gave me a giant hug, and stepped out into the light towards the stage.

I started to follow her out, and stopped just short of the light from the auditorium.

I remained in the shadows and scanned the crowd for Sue's parents, Don and Jackie. Just as Sue reached the stage and began mounting the steps, I spotted them.

The Andersons weren't the flashy type. They weren't holding up a poster bearing Sue's name, and wouldn't be caught dead whistling or screaming across the room. They remained seated, and clapped as their oldest daughter took her place in front of the podium.

Don was a strong, hulking man. He played football in his younger years, and even made the All-American team out of college. He had an impeccable head of hair and still maintained his sleeve-stretching biceps.

Jackie was thin and cheerful. Her smile, much like her daughter's, could silence a room. She overdosed on jewelry, but looked every bit the part of a trophy wife. I knew better though. She was beautiful, but she'd also been head of her class at Stanford and a remarkable thought leader in solar energy. She had emailed me several times to discuss Sue's future.

Don and Jackie sat patient in the front row, Sue's sister Sam just to their left. Sam's brown hair opposed the radiant blonde hair of her sister, but curled the same and flanked her face perfectly. While she sat, she folded her program into a neat origami crane. But even in her fervor, she looked up every few seconds to make sure she wouldn't miss her sister's speech. Sam and Sue, while four years apart, were close. They had their

15

differences, like any siblings, but Sam respected Sue and was proud to witness her graduation.

The Anderson family was an attractive quartet. Yet even though they looked like they stepped out of a magazine cover, they were just as down-to-earth as you could want. Don volunteered at the free clinic whenever he had an off day at his practice. Jackie, while busy herself, still made time to pack both her daughters' lunches and go to every one of their various events.

I watched them wait patiently for Sue to begin from my place in the shadows, admiring their composure. My family was far from put together and I suppose I envied the Andersons. I shifted uncomfortably at this thought when Sue stepped up to the podium. She adjusted the microphone, and it shot loud screaming feedback through the speakers and into the crowd.

Her hands shook and she mumbled an apology as she organized the note cards. Even from my vantage point, I saw the crowd of students had all stopped what they were doing, waiting attentively for Sue to speak. I wondered what they would take away from her words. I hadn't read her speech, but I had a gut feeling that she would blow everyone away.

Sue finished packing her notecards into a tight little pile, and tapped the microphone as if to test it was actually on.

"I've always wanted to do that," she said. This was met with a smattering of laughter from the crowd. Don and Jackie beamed with pride.

It was at that moment that something amazing happened. All of Sue's nerves melted away, and she assumed the role of Sue Anderson: Valedictorian. She was poised; her smile could stop wars. She stood straight, and as she started to speak, she looked directly towards the breezeway where I was quietly tucked away. I was lost in admiration of this wonderful creature.

"It would probably be awfully cliché of me to stand in front of all of my peers with a prepared speech, only to feel compelled to gallantly toss it aside and speak from the heart..." As she said this, she tossed her notecards to the ground, eliciting a standing ovation from several of the graduating seniors.

Sue stood quietly, her eyes darting around the room as if she was deciding what to do next. I looked towards Don and Jackie who were whispering to each other, still looking very proud and attentive. Then, just as the applause had died down, Sue casually reached into the sleeve of her gown and pulled out a fresh set of notecards.

I let loose an audible sigh of relief. It wasn't that I didn't think she was capable of rolling out an inspiring speech on the fly; it was the fact that I'd just spent the last fifteen minutes calming her down. The Sue that stood on the stage now looked nothing like the whimpering girl that had nearly passed out in the breezeway. Had she tricked me?

The crowd was now bewildered, and sat even more attentive, some giggling, while others clapped here and there at her cleverness.

"You didn't really think I was going to throw caution to the wind like that? Of course I prepared something. I graduated high school with honors and a perfect grade point average. It is in my nature to be prepared. But I am not up here to talk about myself. I am here to talk about potential, possibility, promise, and a plethora of other "P" words that may come up.

"Every single person in this room, mainly those that are currently dressed in cap and gown, is here for a reason. You are transitioning. Your life as a high school student and as a teenager, to a certain extent, is over. Let that sink in for a moment. Everyone around us at this very moment, whether they be parents, grandparents, aunts, uncles, teachers, administrators or principals, are expecting us to now be adults. Adults! A dirty four letter word if only it didn't have two extra letters.

"At one point or another, all of us have fantasized about being an adult. Getting that dream job, buying a house, starting a family, drinking wine on the porch of our beach house. Possibilities."

The last word she spaced out more eloquently than William Shatner could ever dream. She was rolling now, and had the attention of the entire auditorium.

"But the truth is, being an adult is not easy. In fact, most days it is downright hard. Today probably spells relief for some of your parents out there. A child graduating high school, affirmation that you didn't to-tally screw up your kid."

The crowd ate this up. Several parents looked at one another, nodding in agreement and smiling. She had hooked them in, and now could pretty much tell them anything she wanted and they would be all ears.

"Four years of high school, for some of us, has seemed like a lifetime. Forgive my further clichés, but many of us will forge friendships here that will last for our entire lives. That is not a small thing. As we have grown into young adults in the halls of William How-ard Taft High School, we have made lots of decisions about ourselves: who we want to spend our time with, our religious beliefs, political affiliation, and ideas about careers. We chose our sexual partners, we decid-ed whether or not to experiment with drugs, alcohol, the length and color of our hair, the list goes on and on.

"High school is our chance to find out what our life is all about, to discover freedom and to make choices that will ultimately affect our lives forever. This is our chance to identify our capabilities, and act on them. Potential.

"Finally, I will leave you with a promise. Mind you, I don't claim to know it all, in fact, I bring this up in the hopes that someone later will approach me and set me straight, passing along the secrets of life. Don't worry, I won't be holding my breath." Sue took in a large deep breath, and held it with puffed out cheeks for what seemed like an eternity. Then, in a pure bit of overacting, she spit out her breath and heaved for air.

"Yes, definitely not going to hold my breath. Anyway, where was I? Right...advice. The world is an ugly place, and every one of us here has already seen glimpses of it. Whether it is on TV or in the news, there are bad people out there doing awful things. And I am afraid the odds are, there is at least one awful person in this very graduating class."

At this, she scanned the crowd and looked in the direction of her friends Ann and Rachel. They were as attentive as the rest of the class, but still managed a wry smile when she looked at them. At this point, I had slumped against the wall, almost as if I were curled up on my couch watching a thriller or action film.

"My promise to you is simple," she continued. "I will wake up every morning. I will live my life, and it will take paths I never dreamed of, but at the end of the day, I will try my hardest to not become one of those bad people. Life is too short to be filled with hate or judgment. Right now, we are seniors. We rule the school. After today, we are merely tadpoles in an enormous ocean. Let's be the best damn tadpoles we can be! Thank you, Taft."

And at that, she slipped in front of the podium and hastily gathered as many of the notecards she had spilled for effect as she could. As she did this, the crowd erupted in applause. Don and Jackie were now wiping proud tears from their eyes, and some of the students were shouting various affirmations toward the stage. A few minutes later, the auditorium had gone quiet as Principal Stevenson directed the other teachers on the stage to begin the handing out of diplomas.

I had seen what I came to see, so I headed down the breezeway looking for an exit. Eventually, after passing quiet restrooms and an endless amount of vacant concession stands, I managed to find a door that led outside. The new spring heat beat down and I immediately shed my jacket and wandered to find my car among the hundreds that now flanked the arena.

It took a good ten minutes to find my aging grey Saturn SL2. When I did finally settle into the driver's seat, I let out a deep breath. I was really going to miss Sue. I thought about the hug she had given me just before her speech. It was one of the most genuine embraces I had had in years.

I turned the ignition to kick on the air conditioner and sat for a moment reflecting on the last two years of Sue Anderson. Was I one of the bad people she'd spoken about?

Never in my entire career had I thought about a student romantically. But there was something about the way she had looked at me. It almost felt like she was in love. The thought made me nervous. I sat in my car worried for some time. I began to hear the rumblings of the crowd heading outside.

Graduation was over. Would I ever see her again? I reached for the door handle more than once as I considered pushing through the crowd to find her, but eventually, I settled on putting the car into drive and slipping out of the parking lot, before the lanes were choked with traffic.

I never saw Sue in the flesh again after that day, though I often thought I spotted her in a bookstore or the grocery store. But it was never her. I imagined that, at some point, her name would show up in a magazine or on the news for some amazing achievement she had managed, but that never happened either.

I went back to Taft that fall, and was once again met with a whole new crop of students, some eager, some flippant, but none compared to the ravishing Sue Anderson.

And for that I was grateful.

CHAPTER TWO
Charlie 1999

My parents named me Charles Thomas Finch. My Grandmother called me Charlie until the day she passed away. That also happened to be the day I received my acceptance letter to college. For me, at the time, getting into college was a bit of a miracle. I became the first of my family to attend, and coming from the small town of Henryetta, Oklahoma, where no one did anything, I considered this a feat.

Most of my friends had already resigned themselves to live and die in a small town. The few that did get out and go to college, usually never ventured further than Tulsa. So when I told everyone that I got accepted to Northwestern University just outside of Chicago, it was like I became a stranger to them.

The weeks leading up to my first day at school were very much a time of solitude. It's funny how easily country folks can turn their backs on the city. Of course my parents were supportive and didn't complain too much when I told them I intended to drive to school on my own. I explained that it would save them gas money and I would be home at Christmas. That was the last I heard of the matter.

The day I left, only one of my friends stopped by to say goodbye. It definitely hurt, but at the same time reinventing myself in Evanston became a top priority. I made the uneventful trip up to school in record time. I wasn't interested in taking it slow. The all-night trip set my mind at ease. In a whirlwind drive filled with beef jerky, Cherry Coke and the oatmeal cookies my mother had packed up neatly for me, I finally arrived in my new home.

I spent the first night on my twin-sized bunk in my new dorm room, staring up at the ceiling, wondering what was in store for me. Meeting my roommate was the next step, but in the three days leading up to the start of classes, he had yet to arrive. Not knowing who he was made me anxious, but it also let me focus on exploring the school and finding all my classrooms.

It was on one of these expeditions that I first met Sue Anderson. I went to check out the boathouse and skip a few rocks into Lake Michigan, which was the closest thing to the ocean I had seen. On my way back to the dorm, I caught sight of a gorgeous girl striding past Fisk Hall. Her auburn hair was glowing like the sun and her dress floated unguarded in the breeze. The sight of her stopped me in my tracks.

She was struggling with several over-sized lollipops in each arm. As she made her way up towards the theater building, she approached me without so much as a glimpse. My entire body tracked hers, as if it were being turned on a spike. The sidewalk narrowed as she got closer. When she was within a few feet of me, she stumbled and the lollipops shifted awkwardly in her arms. A few hit the pavement, bouncing in all directions.

I sprang into action, chasing the wayward lollipops as they scattered into the grass. The auburn beauty launched herself towards the nearest giant candy.

"Don't worry, I got 'em!" I told her.

"Oh, thank you so much."

I scooped up two of the over-sized candies and approached her with unfounded confidence.

"Charlie," I said.

She cocked her head to the side, confused. "I'm glad you were here, Charlie."

I held out my hand to shake hers.

She grinned at my introduction and then immediately cast a look of disappointment.

"My hands are a little full, remind me to shake your hand later," she said.

"What are these for anyways?"

"We're doing a production of Willy Wonka and the Chocolate Factory this fall, and these are for the set. I've got to get to the theater before I drop them all again."

"Oh right," I said, as I settled the rescued lollipops on top of the pile in her arms.

"Thank you, Charlie." She stood erect and clicked her heels together. She then nodded briefly and shrugged her shoulders before heading off in the direction of the theater.

"You're welcome, girl whose name I don't know," I called after her.

She gingerly spun around and began to walk backwards, blushing.

"It's Sue. See ya around." She winked and continued on her way.

***

For two solid weeks after classes began, I wandered around the theater and art buildings, hoping to bump into Sue again. And for two solid weeks I didn't see her even once in passing. Left to my own devices, I might have become obsessed with seeing, let alone talking to her again. But between classes and studying, I didn't have enough time in the day to track down a girl I barely knew.

Just as I was about to give up, I spotted her reading in the Student Union. I knew it was her immediately. She was sitting at a tiny bar-top table with another girl. They were both heads down in textbooks. Occasionally, one or the other would break away to sip from their coffee before continuing to study.

My palms began to sweat as I tried to think of an excuse to approach them. I took my backpack off and settled into a comfy chair across the room with a good sight line of their table. I sat for a few minutes, devising a plan. The window for these types of things are small, and if I didn't go talk to her that day, chances are I would never have another shot. My eyes bounced nervously around the room in anticipation of what I was about to subject myself to.

Then I stood up and plunged my hand inside my backpack. I reached around for a minute, and quickly pulled out a bag of M&M's. I made my way across the room and, as casually as possible, laid the bag of candy onto the book that Sue was reading. Startled, she looked up with her big doe eyes.

"I think you dropped another prop." I braced myself for awkwardness after that awful pick-up line.

"Charlie! Where have you been? I've been looking all over for you." Sue looked over to get the attention of her counter-part. "Addy, this is the Charlie I told you about."

Addy looked up just long enough to force a smile and a slight wave, before returning to her book. Sue on the other hand, lit up. She appeared to be genuinely happy to see me.

Had she really been keeping an eye out for me? Had I managed to make a lasting impression on her?

"Well here I am. Must be your lucky day." My heart sank at the cheese oozing from my mouth, and I tried not to flinch as the sentence rolled off my tongue.

"Indeed it is Charlie. Indeed it is. So what's going on? How are you enjoying this lovely day at Northwestern?"

"Not bad, not bad. Definitely puts Oklahoma to shame, but it's starting to feel normal. How about you?

Are you a freshman? Is that the most common question in the world?"

"That I am, and assuming you are, we should have a lot in common right?"

"So you're majoring in photo-realistic bio-mechanical fashion too?" I offered emphatically.

Without missing a beat Sue took a giant breath and reached out her arms for a hug, "They told me I was one of only two students who picked that major! Are you super excited for the end of semester fashion show?"

Sue, in those few seconds, showed me she could handle my sense of humor. She drew me in, I was engulfed by her. I glanced at the clock to find my next class was about to start. I didn't want to leave.

"Almost as excited as I am for Third Eye Blind this weekend. You guys going?" For me this was as far out on a limb as I could go. I never was good at asking girls out, but Sue was worth the potential beatdown.

"I'll be there. My R.A. had two tickets she couldn't use, so I jumped on them," she said.

"Oh yeah? That's cool. Maybe we can hang out before or something," I said coolly.

Sue hesitated for a moment. I peeked at the clock again waiting for her to decline the invite. I was definitely going to be late for class.

"I'm not sure exactly what the plan is, but we can figure something out. Want to meet us in front of Lutkin Hall around five?"

I suppressed what would have been a very audible sigh of relief. "Sounds good. Okay, well I'm late for class, but we...will...see you later." I finished the sentence by shooting her with a playful gun made out of my hand, a decision I immediately wished I could take back. I turned and walked away forcing myself to not look back.

Sue called out, "See ya later, Charlie," as I nearly fell over some girl in a wheelchair to wave to Sue one last time. I had to get out of there before I made myself even less desirable than I felt.

***

We did end up meeting in front of Lutkin Hall for the concert. Only she came alone because Addy had a migraine and didn't want to get out of bed.

That was the beginning of my relationship with Sue.

After the show, we spent seven hours in a diner asking each other everything, from our opinions on The Cold War to hypothesizing on what we'd do if Jurassic Park was a real amusement park (we both would totally go). To say I was falling in love might have seemed rash, but it wasn't too far from the truth.

Just sitting in the same booth with her changed me into something I can't even describe. It was like that moment when you are little and it dawns on you for the first time that there is a whole world beyond your room, your house, even your planet. It's heavy shit. Sue was heavy and I wanted to feel that way all day long. I should have known it wouldn't last.

My roommate, Carl, eventually moved in, but he soon pledged a fraternity so I barely saw him. Sue and I began the habit of making out in my dorm room. I was very conscious of not putting pressure on her to have sex, but by Halloween I was starting to think something wasn't right. It didn't feel like we were progressing towards anything. That's when I came up with the idea for a trip.

Sue agreed. It was the first time we spent the night together alone. I'd slept over at her place few times, but Addy always seemed to be lingering about. We never managed more than quietly making out in the middle of the night or engaging in some intense spooning.

I targeted the weekend before Thanksgiving for our trip. Sue wanted to go somewhere close enough to drive to, and asked only one thing of me. She wanted to see some art. We settled on visiting the Walker Art Center in Minneapolis. Sue didn't have a car, so we would make the trip in my faded gold, and slightly scary, 1991 Honda Accord.

In the weeks leading up to the trip, Sue had grown increasingly busy. The public TV station, where she worked, was gearing up for their annual donor drive. She would often call and say she was staying at her dorm to catch up on a paper or tackle reading she had fallen behind on.

One night, during one of these phone calls, I told her I loved her. It was a simple declaration and I tried to mask it in a compliment, but I could feel her hesitation through the phone.

"Charlie, yeah. I love you too. But what I'd really love is to move out of the dorms next semester. The community bathroom is really taking its toll."

I got off the phone dejected. I wanted Sue to be the girl that I ended up with. The type of girl I always pictured as a part of my future.

Sue embodied all of these great things in my mind. She did yoga in her free time. She always talked about wanting to learn the guitar, but didn't own one. Once she confessed to me that she was really a blonde and had dyed her hair darker before coming to school. Like me, she was looking to reinvent herself. Sue graduated high school in the top of her class, but she wasn't as nerdy as you would expect. Even so, I was constantly intimidated by her intellect.

The next day, she told me she loved me a few times, almost in passing, but I clung to those words. They echoed through my head as I slept restlessly for the next few nights. By the time the weekend of our trip arrived, I managed to push the word 'love' out of my head. We were going to spend a solid seventy-two hours together and I was looking forward to it more than anything.

Right after class that Friday, I threw my duffle bag into the trunk of the car and drove over to Sue's dorm. I parked outside and leaned against the car, acting as cool as possible while waiting for her. Twenty minutes later, she came bursting out of the building with her backpack on and several books in her arms. She pulled her ponytail out from under one of the straps of her pack as she walked towards me.

"I'm sorry, I'm sorry. I was studying and lost track of time. You ready?" She leaned in and sort of gave me a side hug, as I rested against the car. My cool act was lost on her. She walked around to the other side of the car and tossed her books in the back before jumping in. I stood there for a moment watching her, before climbing in and starting the engine.

It was roughly six and a half hours from Evanston to Minneapolis and I had burned a handful of CDs for the trip. My plan was to subtly remind Sue through music just how much I loved her and hope it was enough to convince her to love me back. I'd already filled the car up with gas, so we hit the highway and headed off into the great unknown of our relationship.

For the first thirty minutes, we sat in awkward silence. Sue picked at the hair on her forearm and occasionally dug in her purse for some phantom object. After I couldn't stand the silence anymore, I tried to force a conversation.

"You know, if we like Minneapolis enough, we could run away there and never come back. I could get a job at a gallery and you could work at a TV station. How much do you think apartments cost there? Probably a lot less than Chicago."

Sue sat quietly. I couldn't decide if she was intentionally ignoring me or not, but it was driving me crazy.

"Sue, you alright?"

"What? Charlie, I'm fine. I just had a long day is all. Can we turn on some music or something?"

I nodded and reached for my curated road trip CDs. I popped one in the CD player and Fiona Apple came floating out of the speakers. Sue loved Fiona Apple. I found her music to be quite depressing and it always put me in a bad mood, but if it helped make Sue feel more relaxed it was worth a shot.

She smiled slightly and closed her eyes as Fiona's vocals drove *Fast As You Can* throughout the car. Eventually, Sue drifted off to sleep. The soundtrack of my love for her played for the next forty-five minutes. She didn't hear a thing.

Just as the sun set, I nudged her awake to ask if we should stop somewhere for dinner. She tugged on her t-shirt, causing her bra to show itself for a brief moment. She stretched across the roof of the car as she nodded and yawned at the same time.

We were on an old country highway at this point, so the chance of finding a romantic place to stop for dinner was a joke. We settled on a small diner just outside of Janesville, Wisconsin. Sue's spirits seemed to have lifted as the waitress brought us matching plates of French toast and scrambled eggs. We clanged our forks together, I faked a smile, and we toasted the trip before drenching our meals in syrup.

I devoured my egg-coated Texas toast in massive bites to avoid a direct conversation. When I finished, my empty plate looked sad. I picked at the few scraps that remained with my fork. The whole trip was a mistake. Nothing felt right. I didn't know what else to do, so I started small. I leaned across the table and whispered to Sue.

"Do you ever tell people I'm your boyfriend?" I asked.

"What do you mean?" she said. She set her fork down and took a sip of her orange juice while she stared vacantly out the window.

"I'm your boyfriend, right?"

"Well I mean, yeah I guess so. Are you feeling insecure?"

Sue had a way of looking at things through a funnel of neurosis. If she didn't want to answer a question or have a conversation, she would just throw a diagnosis at you. She would always accuse me of having ADHD or bi-polar disorder if she didn't feel like fighting over the remote control or choosing a place to go to dinner. It was obvious she didn't want to talk about our relationship.

I clinched my teeth and took short breaths through my nostrils. She guessed so? What was that supposed to mean? I excused myself and wandered off to find the restroom. As soon as I went around the corner, I pulled my hand hard through my hair. I was convinced it was over.

When I came back, Sue had paid the check and was waiting in the car for me. She had barely touched her food. I didn't quite know what to make of the move, but it was getting late and I just wanted to go to sleep. I hadn't made hotel reservations, though. When I planned the trip, I figured it would be more fun to choose a place once we got there, a decision I was already regretting.

When I got into the car, she was gleefully organizing my belongings in the glove box, her attempt to make me feel better. She had one of my road trip CDs in the player and had cranked up the volume. She was singing and bobbing her head to *Kiss Me* by Sixpence None The Richer. Kissing her was the only thing I wanted to do. Watching her sing made my stomach hurt.

I buckled my seat belt and turned the ignition, but I only heard a clicking noise. I tried again with the same result. I could feel panic building inside of me. Nothing makes a person feel more hopeless than their car not starting hours away from home. That and the feeling of breaking up with your girlfriend.

I tried a few more times to no avail. I pounded on the steering wheel, growing more and more frustrated. My first instinct was to apologize to Sue. I had planned this whole trip for her and now it was in shambles.

I went through our options in my head. The first was obvious, call a tow truck to take us to a repair shop. I didn't have the money and it was getting late. Then I considered popping the hood to check if anything looked amiss, maybe a loose wire or a dead bird, something I could fix. I asked Sue if she had any suggestions. She offered to go find a phone and some yellow pages.

Just as I was about to agree, I took one more shot at the ignition. Much to our surprise the car rumbled to life. We both looked at each with a glimmer of victory in our eyes. Maybe the trip was starting to go my way after all. There was only one way to find out. I would put it in her hands.

"What do you want to do? I'm not sure its gonna start again. We might be better off just going home."

She propped her leg up on the dashboard and started pulling her hair up in a ponytail, something she often did when she wanted to concentrate on something. The weight of my world hung on her next words.

"We've already come this far, let's throw caution to the wind. I really want to see the art center." She wrapped her hands around my arm, trying to assure me we would come out on the other side unscathed. While I had my doubts, I leaned in closer to her and then threw the car in drive, heading toward Minneapolis.

The remainder of the drive was rather uneventful. Still, in the back of my mind, I couldn't shake what Sue had said about being my girlfriend. But, as long as the car was running, I had something else to focus all my anxiety on. I decided it was only a matter of time before we would have to deal with that problem.

Sue was much more attentive on this leg of the trip. It was as if she had a weight lifted off her shoulders. We talked about a dream she'd had the night before, where she was stuck in an elevator with John Travolta and Gene Simmons from KISS. She managed to talk them into arm wrestling, but woke up before she found out who won. We figured it was probably Travolta.

The air outside was cool as we motored down the highway, but that didn't stop Sue from rolling down the window. She leaned her head out like an excited dog, pushing her face into the breeze and shifting in her seat to rest her feet in my lap. It was all I could do to concentrate on the road.

The rest of the drive we sang and laughed. It was everything I had hoped for when I asked her to come with me. I thought, maybe Sue was the one for me after all. I was riding the high of that thought as we rolled into downtown Minneapolis on fumes.

We scouted a small motel near a gas station. It was only a short walk to the art museum so we headed inside to grab a room for the night.

The lobby was very small, a bit dark and smelled like mustard. It was close to eleven o'clock at night, so the place was nearly deserted as we approached the counter. A small woman in an oversized cardigan sweater hovered near a computer monitor.

"Good evening." she greeted us with a bit of a snort. Her dark brown hair was awkwardly clipped several times over to the side. She focused her attention on me, but before I could speak, Sue did.

"We'd like a room for the night. Two queens, if you got it?" I felt awkward so I crouched down below the desk and pretended to look for something in my bag. Why would Sue want two beds? I tried not to think about it as Sue paid for the room and we made our way back outside. It was getting late and I was more than ready to kick off my shoes and crash.

We pushed our way into the dark room with our bags draped over our shoulders like sleeping cats. I dumped my stuff on the first of the two queen sized beds as fast as I could. Much to my surprise, Sue tossed her bag onto the same bed. Now I was completely confused.

"Do you need in the bathroom?" I asked. "I'm gonna freshen up a bit if you don't mind."

"Nope, go for it."

I grabbed a small lunch baggie containing my toothbrush and a few other hygiene items and ducked into the bathroom. I didn't bother shutting the door while I fumbled with the toothpaste. As I brushed my teeth, I stood and stared into the mirror. It had been a long day, a roller coaster of feelings, at least from my perspective. I had no clue what Sue was thinking, but I was hell-bent on finding out.

I leaned out the door and saw Sue changing out of her shirt. Her back faced me. She had already removed her bra, her bare back was extremely inviting. I wanted nothing more than to run my hands down her smooth skin. As I imagined rushing to her side, she turned to face me, her breasts exposed. She stood, unabashedly, as the moonlight poking through the window cast an oblong shadow over her shoulder.

I stood dumbstruck with my toothbrush hanging out of my mouth. Her beauty literally stunned me and I couldn't move. She made eye contact and we held the stare for a few moments, neither of us saying a word. Finally, Sue threw her shirt over her head and I retreated back to the bathroom to rinse out my mouth. I did this fast, in the event there was an intimate moment to be had in the other room.

When I finally made my way out to the beds, Sue had already climbed under the covers of first bed. Our bags were now on the floor. I had a decision to make. Do I crawl into bed with her or take the other bed?

But I wanted answers. I needed to know where Sue and I stood. Was this trip all for nothing? Was our relationship doomed? I gathered in a fair amount of bravery and nestled into bed, right next to her. She didn't make a move and just lay there with her back to me. I held steady for a second on my elbow, waiting. When she didn't budge, I threw myself on my back and let out an audible sigh. I shriveled under my own anxiety.

"Hey? Can we talk?" I said.

"Yep."

"I guess I wanted this trip so you and I could get closer and...I guess...get more serious about being together. But so far, it kind of feels all over the place. It's making my head spin."

She lay quietly in the dark. I could hear the pace of her breathing. It was almost as if she was thinking of just the right thing to say.

After an agonizingly long time, she spoke.

"Charlie, I really do care about you, but...," she started. I quietly sucked in as much air as I could and mumbled "but" under my breath.

"But, I have a lot going on and I need to worry about me. I know that sounds callous and maybe a little mean, but I'm just not sure that I can give you what you need right now."

"What do you think I need?" My voice was trembling now.

"The one," she said.

"Sue, if 'the one' is even a real thing, it would definitely be you. Please know that. But, I've noticed the last couple of weeks you haven't been all there." My eyes started to water. I was glad the room was dark, so she couldn't see what a blubbering mess I was about to become. I tried to focus on short steady breaths, anything to calm me down.

"I don't think I'd make a very good girlfriend now. I'd let you down and I don't want you to hate me." She turned to face me and I could see the silhouette of her head and shoulders against the motel window. Her hot breath sunk into my skin as she spoke.

I took her face in my hands. "Sue, I love you. That should be all that matters."

"Charlie, don't." She pulled away.

"Don't what? I know what we have is real. I know you can feel it too. Don't give up on this. On us. Please."

"I just need to focus on other things right now." She took my hands away from her face and pulled them into her lap. She held onto them tightly, squeezing my fingers together. "I still want you in my life. I don't want to lose you."

Her words-I don't want to lose you-filled my throat with a bile taste. This was the girl I loved, but she was keeping me at arm's length. She held me back, but wouldn't let me go.

"Is there someone else?" I said.

"Charlie, no. It's not like that."

I took a deep breath, realizing as I did I was clutching my sheets into a ball. I sat upright on the bed. Embarrassed, and on the verge of tears, I decided to protect myself.

"Sue, let's just forget it." I threw one leg over the side of the bed and shifted my body away from her. "I can't wait for you to fall in love with me. If you don't think I'm something you can commit to, I'll just let you off the hook. You don't have to be my girlfriend anymore. I'm not going to force you to love me, it doesn't work that way. Maybe you'll change your mind someday, but I'd be an asshole if I waited around for it to happen."

Sue sat up and scooped her knees to her chest. She didn't seem like she was going to say anything.

Above all, that hurt the most. She wasn't going to fight for our relationship.

When she finally did say something, it was soft and masked by tears. I strained to hear her as she simply said, "Sorry."

"I'm exhausted, I'm going to sleep." I moved over to the other bed and scrambled under the covers.

She sat still for a while longer and finally I could hear her breathing slow down as she drifted off to sleep.

I lay awake for another hour, tears in my eyes. I'd just lost the love of my life. I would have been a fool to chase after her with nothing to gain. I made the mature move, but in the moment, I felt like a loser. It was close to four in the morning before I dozed off, my face hot with grief.

In the morning we dressed in silence and made our way down to grab breakfast at a diner across the street. After a while conversation began to pick up. Before we made it to the art museum, we had shoved our quasi-breakup to the back of our minds. We were once again two peas in a pod. Still, occasionally I found myself overcome with a wave of sadness.

Where was her life taking her that didn't include me? I had no way of knowing. I only knew that every time my hand brushed against hers or I looked into her eyes, I could feel that she wasn't mine anymore. She never would be.

When we left the art museum, we made the mutual decision to just drive home. In the state my car was in, there were a limited number of chances it would actually start successfully. We stopped at a gas station to fill up the tank and grab some provisions for the ride home.

Sue slept the majority of the way. The silence was irritating. I wanted to hate her so much for not wanting to give us a chance. But I couldn't, even if I tried. She was as angelic as ever, slumped against the window, softly breathing hot air onto the glass.

When we finally made it back to campus, I pulled up to the curb in front of her dorm. She stirred herself awake as I came to a complete stop. She stretched her arms and yawned. As she worked herself fully awake, she began looking around the car for her things, then leaned in close to me and kissed me on the cheek.

"I had a good time, Charlie. Thank you for taking me."

"Me too," I lied.

As she climbed out of the car clutching her things, she turned and poked her head back inside.

"I'll talk to you soon, okay?"

"Yeah, sure. Take care," I said.

I watched her walk the long sidewalk to the front of her dormitory. Once she was inside and out of sight, I casually smashed my head into the steering wheel. I sat there for a few minutes, resisting the urge to weep. Eventually, I put the car in drive and made my way home.

That was the last time I really felt close to her. I made feeble attempts to keep her in my life, but she was always too busy to make it work. We passed each other on campus a few times, but things never felt the same after our trip. We didn't talk on the phone. She never showed up at my door to study, or with a movie in hand, hoping to cuddle on my bed.

By spring break, she had become invisible. I stopped hoping I would see her as I passed from one end of the campus to the other.

In May, a few weeks before finals, I bumped into Addy as I came out of one of my classes.

"Charlie, hey."

"What's up, Addy? You and Sue staying out of trouble?"

She looked at me with a puzzled look in her eyes.

"Is everything okay?" I asked.

"Oh shit. Charlie, I thought you knew."

"What are you talking about?"

"Sue got really sick. She went back home to live with her parents a few months ago. She's been going back and forth to the doctor. They still don't know what's wrong, but it's pretty serious. I thought she'd have told you."

Why hadn't she said anything? It was clear we had both moved on, but something still made me feel like she would have told me something big like that. I tried not to think too much into it.

"Is she going to be alright? I don't even know how to get a hold of her."

"I hope so. I talk to her every few days to see if they've figured anything out. I have her parents' number in my room if you want to stop by sometime and get it. I'm sure she'd love to hear from you."

"Yeah, I'll do that." I looked at the clock on the wall behind me. "Listen, I gotta run. Good seeing you and thanks for the heads up. If you talk to her before I do, tell her that I...tell her I hope she's okay."

Addy nodded and we went our separate ways. All my emotions for Sue rushed back. She was sick and I didn't even know about it. My heart ached and I couldn't think straight. I went back to my room and collapsed on my bed.

I stayed in that night, enjoying the quiet and watching old TV shows on my laptop. Before I knew it, finals were in full force and I never quite made the time to stop by Addy's room to get the number for Sue's parents. This was, ultimately, my greatest regret in life. Sue Anderson was in my life for a brief, brief time and I let her slip away. I should have called her. Hell, I should have gotten in my car and driven to her side, but I lacked the courage and the resolve.

Would it have made a difference, my showing back up in her life? Would she have taken my hand and squeezed it tight? Would we have spent the night wrapped in each other's arms? I will never know. That is not my story, and Sue Anderson is not my happy ending.

CHAPTER THREE
Samantha 2000

I was putting the finishing touches on my sophomore year of high school when Sue came back home to stay. She insisted everything was fine at school and didn't want to come home while the doctors tried to fix her. But Mom and Dad wanted to keep her close by so they could go to appointments with her and make sure nothing bad happened.

The whole thing made me nervous. She already collapsed a few times at school. No one was saying it out loud, but it seemed pretty freaking serious. The last time she fell, she split her head open falling down a long flight of concrete stairs.

That's when everyone agreed she had to come home.

She insisted it was just the flu or something. She was always coming up with normal reasons for the fainting. She blamed it on her studies or her ex-boyfriend.

Whatever it was, it had me worried, though I never came right out and told her that. It was a relief when she told my parents she would come home from school three weeks early.

It was the topic of conversation when she called home. She would go on and on how her stupid sickness was getting in the way of her schoolwork, but I could hear it in her voice, in the background, she was freaking out.

"I'm too tired to do anything, Sam. I get dizzy too. But I'm sure it'll pass someday. I'm probably not eating properly. I've almost hit my freshman fifteen, so I probably should fix that."

On the weekend Sue came home, both my parents had driven down to pick her up. Mainly because my Dad didn't want Sue to drive herself home, so my Mom drove Sue home in Sue's car and Dad drove in his. When she walked into the house, she didn't look sick at all. I wondered if she was just messing with us, maybe she wanted to stretch her summer break a little longer?

But I knew that something wasn't right. The first thing she did was immediately give me the biggest and warmest hug I think I'd ever gotten from her. Her face was buried into my shoulder and she lingered for what seemed like an eternity.

As far as sisters go, we were close, but hugging wasn't something we did unless we knew we weren't going to see each other for a very long time. As a greeting, it was kind of strange.

She was sincerely happy to see me, not that she shouldn't be, but the hug had set a weird tone in the room and it made it all more awkward.

"Thanks, I guess." I said as I pulled out of the hug.

"It's good seeing you too, Sam." She nodded and gave me a soft smile.

"I know. How ya feeling?"

"Never been better." She trembled a bit as she said it, but I didn't let on I knew she was lying.

All in all, I didn't mind having Sue home. She and I got along. Since our parents worked a lot, she practically raised me. She was just enough older than me that I still looked up to her, and she never acted superior. She treated me as an equal when we hung out.

Once Sue got settled in, it turned out there wasn't a lot for her to do. She was so far ahead in most of her classes, a lot of her professors showed sympathy and let her skip finals and gave grades based on her completed work. Like the nerd she was, she felt extremely guilty about it.

Because of her lack of anything school related, she spent a lot of time with me, laying by the pool soaking up the sun or reading. Physically, she still looked healthy, even if she was often fatigued.

Looking at us, Sue and I were definitely sisters. We had similar thin frames and a skin tone that our mother called Italian envy.

Sue, however, was definitely a much more matured version of myself. She was the type of girl that never really worked out, but was always active, and it showed. Her bikini filled out in all the right places.

Sue wasn't without her flaws. When she sneezed, it was sort of a half sneeze. It drove me crazy, she had the *ah, ah,* but never the *choo.* Her socks never matched either. She would say sorting them was a waste of time. She would leave toothpaste in the sink, drink the last of the O.J. and leave the container in the fridge. I could go on and on. Regardless, she could definitely turn heads, unlike me.

As soon as she got home she began eating very healthy, which really annoyed me. She must have thought it would help counter whatever it was that was screwing with her.

It was almost summer break and all I cared to do was veg out by the pool and eat junk food, so Sue's health kick was more or less annoying.

About a week after Sue's return, my Mom told me I had to drive Sue to the doctor. Basically anywhere she needed to go, I was her chauffeur, because they were afraid of her passing out behind the wheel.

The last thing I wanted to do was waste my time driving around my older sister, who was perfectly capable of driving herself.

That summer was supposed to be my summer of discovery, not my summer of taxiing Sue from place to place.

Sue tried to be really polite about it though, and after the first week I had forgotten I was supposed to be annoyed. It gave me something to do and I felt like I was in the inner circle of her pending diagnosis. When we would leave a doctor's office, I'd grill her on everything that happened. I wanted to be the first to know what was wrong with her.

"When do you get the results of your latest blood work? Have they ruled out cancer? Can you feel your feet?" These questions would last the whole drive home and sometimes I would forget where we were driving to, ending up all over the place.

It was going on almost two months since Sue had first started to get fatigued and dizzy at school. She had gone through all sorts of lab work and stress tests. And during dinner, a family dinner where all four of us happened to be home at the same time, the phone finally rang.

Our Dad answered the phone initially, but didn't waste any time passing the phone to Sue. She shifted in her seat to take the call, so her back was facing the rest of the family.

"Hello? Hello, Dr. Norris. Yes. Oh I'm hanging in there." She started twirling her hair around her index finger and took a few long deep breaths. "What does that mean exactly?"

My Mom stood up to move closer to Sue, but my Dad grabbed her arm and with his eyes told her to sit down. She paused for a moment and then settled back to the edge of her chair, leaning closer to Sue as if she was straining to hear the doctor's voice.

"That sounds serious." Her back was turned, but we could see she was bouncing her left leg up and down like a paint shaker at a hardware store. "No, I think I'm fine. I guess it's nice to finally know what's wrong. Ok, yeah that should be fine. I'll come prepared with questions. Yes. Okay. Thank you, Dr. Norris. See you then."

Sue hung up the phone and spun around in her chair. For a moment she didn't do anything. She didn't look at any of us. She just sat there, completely inside of herself.

"Honey, what did the doctor say?" My Mother asked.

Sue sucked in a heavy breath, "I have...he called it dilated cardiomyopathy. The walls of my heart are thinning and making it hard to properly pump my blood, so that's why I'm so tired and dizzy all the time." She spoke slow and deliberate, I think she didn't want to have to repeat it.

My mom simply gasped and Dad reached across the table to squeeze Sue's hand. "Honey, I love you. Your mother and I will come with you to see the doctor. I'm sure everything will be fine."

My Dad was always cool under pressure. If he was concerned at all, you wouldn't have been able to guess it. Not that he had a heart of stone or anything, he approached everything with a lot more rationale than the rest of us.

I sat there watching Sue, stunned. I wasn't sure how serious cardiomyopathy was, but it seemed pretty damn serious. The whole table fell silent. Mom suddenly got up from the table, only to return with an opened bottle of wine.

Sue's eyes were darting all over the room, like an animal looking for a way out of a cage. When she didn't find one, she settled on pouring herself some wine into her empty water glass. Neither my mom nor my dad stopped her or said anything. It felt like it was her last supper. We all reluctantly finished eating and collectively cleared the table.

I started to head upstairs to my room, when I turned around and gave Sue a hug that surprised us both. I didn't much feel like talking to her, mainly because I had no idea what to say, so I clutched her neck and squeezed. She hugged back and I could feel her slump into me, until I was holding her up almost entirely. She pulled away after a moment and rubbed my back, her way of thanking me.

"Sam, do you think you can help me upstairs? I'm really tired all of a sudden."

I wrapped my arm around her waist and led her up to bed without a word.

***

My whole body pulled to the left and the right as something tugged me awake. It was Sue. She had both her hands across my back, but the effort still felt half-hearted. It startled me none-the-less. I sat myself up onto my elbows, mostly out of fear, to find Sue completely dressed and hovering over me.

"Get dressed. I need a ride."

"What time is it?" I asked.

53

"I'm not sure," She said absentmindedly. "Maybe two or three in the morning?"

I threw myself back onto my pillow and closed my eyes. I could feel Sue, unwavering, above me. I sat up again.

"Are you serious right now?" I said.

"Definitely."

"Okay fine. Where are we going?"

"Just get dressed and meet me downstairs." She made her way out of the room in a slow cadence, as if she was trying to avoid land mines or holes in the ground. I could hear her soft footsteps make their way to the staircase and begin to move down.

I slipped out of bed and fumbled in the dark for a pair of shorts and a t-shirt. I pulled my keys out of my backpack on my desk chair and fell forward into some flip-flops. I turned to look at the clock, which read 2:17, and made my way downstairs to meet Sue.

When I got downstairs, Sue was nowhere. I wandered around the dark house for ten minutes until I finally found her waiting for me in the passenger seat of my car.

"Where are you going?" I said in a hurried tone as I climbed into the car.

"Second star to right and straight on till morning." She stared out the window at the neighbor's cat prowling around the bushes in the front yard.

I considered pressing her for direction, but instead started up the car and pulled out of the driveway.

I figured she just wanted to be alive, to live in that moment. I was kind of glad I was in the car with her.

So in the middle of the night, I drove. I drove and I drove with no rhyme or reason. We passed the W.H. Taft High School, we passed the dress shop where Sue had her first job. We soon found ourselves on a tour of our childhood, remembering places that our parents used to take us when we were young. We mourned spots now torn down and replaced, like Dover's Pizza, which was now a convenience store blasting annoying bright lights into the night.

We drove by our first house on Maxwell Road. We moved away when I was five, so while my memories were a bit foggy, Sue reminded me of all the strange neighbors and the loose brick on the side of the house where we would hide pennies.

As I drove, Sue became less stiff and serious. She was thinking about her life faster than her mouth could speak and what came out was excited and full of giggles.

"Ewww, look! Mark Porter's house. He put his hand up my shirt once during his birthday party. I nearly broke his finger!"

"Right on that corner is where I decided to turn my bike around and come home after trying to ride to the ocean. Mom was super pissed about that one."

"Oh remember that weird carnival that set up right there in front of the hardware store? And we begged Dad to stop so we could pet a llama? And then when we got there, it spit on you!"

I butted in here and there, but mainly listened to story after story come flowing out of Sue's mouth. She had a memory like a steel trap and as she rambled on, I realized I missed my sister. She had only been away at college for ten months, but as we sat there I realized just how much I loved her.

Eventually I found myself driving towards the lake. It was not even four in the morning and the sky was still dark. The park we used to play at as kids wasn't open yet, so I pulled into a clearing near the locked entrance gate. We climbed out of the car and made our way down to the rocky shore. Sue settled down on a large boulder and scooted her body right to the edge of the water.

She chucked a few rocks out into the water as I positioned myself right next to her. It was completely silent at that hour, save for a few crickets and the distant hum of cars on the road behind us. We both leaned back on our elbows, watching the water rise and fall in the subtle breeze.

"I guess I always pictured myself getting married and starting a family down the road. Like I would have plenty of time for all that later. Going to my kid's graduation, watching them get married..." Sue trailed off a bit. "I want that stuff, eventually. I would finish school and become a writer for the Washington Post or something and then find someone that loved me. Now I'll be lucky to make it to Christmas."

"Sue, don't say that. You haven't even talked to the doctor about it. It might not be that big of a deal, right?" I said.

"No, it's true. I looked it up earlier. My heart won't last forever. I'm a ticking bomb."

"Don't jump to conclusions. And stop looking things up online."

"My whole life, my *whole life*, I have tried to do the right thing, stay out of trouble, make Mom and Dad happy. I mean I've always done well in school. They can trust me to make the right decisions. Not a single misstep and this is the thanks I get? It isn't fair. I don't want to die yet." As she spoke her voice grew louder and more defiant. "I won't get to go to Paris now, I'll never live in Brooklyn. I can forget about falling in love...nothing...*poof*."

Hearing her say these things broke my heart, I started sobbing. "I don't...don't want to...lose you Sue." I wanted to say so much more, but my emotions seized up my throat and all I could manage were tears and gasps for air.

I wanted to tell her that she was a better mother than our own. That she was a role model and she was pretty and funny and caring and smart and everything I wanted to be when I got older. But nothing came out of my mouth but uneven air and snot sliding out of my nose and resting against my upper lip. I was a mess. Pushing into her, I settled on nuzzling into her shoulder and erupted into a slobbering mess, crying and crying.

Then it was Sue who was comforting me, and when I realized it, I immediately tried to straighten up and pull myself together. I wasn't the sick one. She needed me to stay strong.

"You know what you need to do, Sue? You need to make a list of things you haven't done but have always wanted to do. This is your chance to get into some shit, go make mistakes, live a little. Mom and Dad would never see it coming." It made perfect sense to me. I didn't want her to miss out on anything.

Sue looked over at me as I wiped some of my tears away. She was smirking as if to tell me that my brilliant plan was stupid. I was the one who got in trouble, I made mistakes, I brought the bad boys home. Sue was always on the right side of the coin.

"Sue, can I ask you something?"

"I don't see why not."

"Have you had sex yet?" It was a very personal question, and it annoyed me I didn't know the answer already. "You don't have to tell me if you don't want."

"Have you, Sam?" she said.

"Well, sort of. I mean, yes. But he didn't last very long and we only did it once."

"With who?"

"Ryan. It was the end of freshman year. We broke up not too long after that."

"Why didn't you tell me?" she said.

"Why would I? I wasn't upset about it. It isn't like he raped me or anything. It was mutual, it just wasn't meant to be is all."

"How cosmopolitan of you, Sam." Sue said.

"And what about you? Have you ever had sex?"

"I should have with Josh in high school, but that's complicated." She paused for a moment to reflect. "And there was Charlie last fall. I almost did before we broke up. We slept naked sometimes, but he never made a move."

"Would you have? With Charlie I mean."

Sue thought for a moment before answering. "Yeah, I think so. He was a decent guy. I don't think I was ready for him and all his feelings. And I was already going to the doctor and starting to feel dizzy a lot. I didn't want to burden him."

"You know what I think?" I asked.

"What?"

"I think you better get on that. You don't want to die a virg..." I stopped myself and instantly felt like a dirtbag.

Sue smacked me playfully in the arm and we both lay back onto the rock in a heap. The sky had turned an odd shade of purple, a sign that morning was right around the corner. But I wasn't ready for the night to end.

I bolted up, took a look around the secluded park and shimmied out of my shirt and shorts. Sue looked at me sideways for a moment, but as I stepped down into the water, she did the same. Before we knew it, we were wading fifteen feet from the shore, the moon diving head first into the other side of the lake.

"Are you sure you are okay? If you get tired let me know and I will take you back to shore." I said.

"Would you stop it? I can almost touch here. I'm fine." She stopped treading water for a second to prove that she could indeed touch the bottom if need be. "Promise me something okay?"

"Anything," I said.

"Promise me that no matter what happens to me or no matter how long I'm around, you follow your dreams and live your life to the fullest."

"That might be the most cliché thing you've ever said." I smiled, trying to take the pressure off the conversation.

My face was suddenly covered in a wave of water. Sue's arms were rearing back to douse me a second time.

"Okay, okay! Sue I promise!" Giggling, I splashed her back, careful to not make her exert too much energy. Over our laughter I shouted, "You have to promise me something too."

"What?" Sue was squinting her eyes to avoid my splash attack.

"Just because you are sick or whatever, doesn't mean you get to give up either." She stopped splashing. "It wouldn't be fair if you gave up on everything because of this," I said.

"Sam..." Sue started.

"Don't Sam me. I didn't say it was going to be easy, but you're smart and pretty and capable of doing anything you put your mind to, so suck it up and live. Promise me?"

Sue spun around in the water a few times, thinking. She looked up into the purple sky and dipped her hair into the water.

"Sue, promise?" I said.

"It would be pretty easy for me to give in and live with Mom and Dad for a while, wouldn't it? Just wither away. It could be a nice change of pace. Not having to live up to anyone's standards, catch up on *Felicity*. That would be the life, huh?" Sue's eyes glazed over a bit, she seemed to be daydreaming.

"Sue..."

"We better get back to the house. Mom will freak out if I'm not there when she wakes up. I don't want them worrying," she said.

I didn't say anything; I was angry that she pushed off my promise. I splashed heavily back to our clothes. As I dressed, I kept a vigilant eye on Sue as she made her way out of the water. She grabbed her clothes and caught me by the shoulder as I finished slipping my feet back into their flip-flops.

"I promise, Sam."

I smiled and gave her a giant hug. As we embraced, I tried really hard to focus on the pounding heart in her chest. I couldn't decide if it seemed different from my own. I decided, probably to make myself feel better, she was going to be fine. Cardiomyopathy or not, she was still my sister and I wasn't ready to say goodbye.

We drove back to the house with only the gentle sounds of soft rock filling our ears. After quietly slipping into the back door by the pool, we crept up the stairs to sneak back into our rooms and back to bed. In a few short hours, Sue would go meet Dr. Norris and get the details on what her heart was doing.

I lay quietly in my room, eyes wide open until I could hear my mom shuffling about in her bedroom. I felt incredibly helpless.

***

After breakfast we all loaded up in Dad's car to see Dr. Norris. My parents were more anxious to visit with the doctor than before. The whole way there was a series of sincere affirmations that Sue was wonderful and strong and nothing could stop her.

Sue muttered the occasional 'thank you' but largely stared out the window, her body frozen with anticipation. She was the last to climb out of the car when we arrived at the office park. My mother offered to get her a wheelchair if she was too fatigued to walk. This must have offended Sue, because she instantly scoffed and charged inside ahead of us.

When we caught up, Sue was resting against the wall by the elevator, clearly winded from her outburst.

"I'm fine, Mom. Just please, don't," Sue said.

Not another word was spoken as we rode the elevator and sat in the waiting room of the cardiologist's office. When the nurse called Sue's name, we all stood up.

I wanted to go back with her, but my mom didn't want Sue to feel overwhelmed. I tried to look to Sue for any signal that it was okay for me to come, but she only turned and followed the nurse through the heavy grey doors which lead to the examination rooms. My parents rushed after her and I was forced to linger in waiting room alone. It killed me.

The waiting room was empty, save for a man who seemed to be pushing about one hundred and thirty. His frail frame fell limp and his hands wobbled wildly as he tried to fill out some forms on a clipboard. I couldn't help but notice his clothes were two sizes too big for him and what remained of his hair was carefully pushed straight back. He looked up suddenly and caught me staring at him.

"Hello there," He muttered.

"Uh, hi." I became sheepish and searched for anything else to look at. I picked up a magazine, hoping to climb inside of it.

"Don't worry sweetheart, you aren't going to break my heart, it is already busted." The skin on his face managed to contort itself into the widest and most genuine smile you could ever imagine as he pointed to his chest. I instinctively smiled back.

"I see what you did there." It was hard not to warm up to this guy, and I even felt a little bad for him.

"Is that your sister you came with?"

"Yeah, how did you know?"

"You gals look like twins. She got a bum ticker too?" He snickered.

"Yeah." I sighed at the thought. Suddenly I felt a pang in my side. My sister was too young to have a bad heart, right? This type of thing was ripe for old guys like this, not Sue.

"Well Dr. Norris is one of the best. I wouldn't be here today if it weren't for him. Your sister is in good hands," he said.

"I hope so...is she going to be okay?" I don't know why I asked him, I figured he must be an expert if he was still moving around at his age.

"Sweetheart, if she is as clever as you, she'll be around for quite some time. If she takes care of herself. It isn't all roses and cream pies though. I've been fighting for five years now. Been through it all. Started with a new diet and mild exercise, that turned into blood thinners and ACE inhibitors, beta-blockers, you name it. I'm sporting this very smart pacemaker now and we are talking about a LVAD today. It's hard sometimes, but worth it. I'm not ready to leave yet."

"What's an LVAD?" I said.

"Some doo-hickey they put in your heart to help pump the old blood." He waved his hands in the air, pushing away nothing. "I stopped reading about it all ages ago, I just listen to the Doc and try not to kill myself." With that he showed his sly grin once more and then closed his eyes and leaned back in his chair.

Was Sue really going to be okay? I sat there a moment wondering whether I should trust the good-natured old dude or wait for the official word from Dr. Norris. Either way, it seemed like Sue was in for a lifetime of medicine and healthy eating, if she stood a chance at all.

While I waited, I stuffed a bunch of informational flyers into my pocket. I was clawing at anything I thought would help.

***

Unfortunately, that visit put a face on Sue's condition, and that was only the beginning. Her overall weakness required bed rest until she was able to proceed with a custom exercise regimen. Then came the medicine supplements. For the rest of the summer, Sue rotated between being stuck in bed or treading water in the pool and other light exercises.

To her credit, she was handling it all very well. Dr. Norris had told her, given her age and ability, it was possible for her to actually strengthen her heart over time. If all went well it could render her symptoms all but forgotten. However, he was quick to remind her that cardiomyopathy never truly disappeared.

When the end of the summer came, along came the discussion as to whether Sue would return to school in the fall. Our parents had become like leeches, clinging to Sue every chance they got. They weren't in love with the idea of her leaving again and suggested she stay home for at least another semester.

She reluctantly agreed, but only on the condition she was finally allowed to drive again. Leading up to September her spirits were high.

Too bad it didn't last very long. It was my first day back at school, and Sue collapsed at the grocery store on one of her first solo trips since she came home. She was rushed to the hospital and endured a ton of tests and a few overnights. In the end, she was put on a few more prescriptions to help control her heartbeat. Once again, my parents restricted her to the house, unless I drove her, which was a lot harder to do once school had started.

One Friday night, a few weeks before Halloween, Sue came into my room. I had been doing homework and didn't notice her at first. She wandered into my room and was fingering the pictures taped to my mirror.

"Sam? Are you happy?"

Startled, I sat up in my bed and stared at her for a moment. She was dressed in dingy pajamas and looked like she hadn't taken a shower in a week.

There was a certain protocol that we had adopted in the house when Sue was acting funny. My mom created a short set of questions we were required to ask Sue. We could never be sure if she was having an episode or was depressed. If she failed them, we might have to rush her to the hospital.

"Sue, do you know where you are?" I asked.

"Sam, cut the shit."

I was honestly a bit relieved when she lashed out at the first question. This meant that she was fine and only feeling a bit down.

"Are you happy? Sue repeated.

"I think so," I answered honestly. Sue moved from the mirror to the bed and began to curl up into a little ball, eventually resting her head in my lap. I fought off the tears building in my eyes and reminded myself of the nice old man at Dr. Norris' office. Sue was going through it all. She was doing everything the doctors asked of her, but it wasn't what she wanted to be doing. She wanted to be living like she was twenty and healthy.

"Listen, it's up to you to be happy. I don't think I have the stomach for it anymore," she said.

"Stop saying that. You're not going anywhere. Your life is waiting for you. You just need to be patient," I said.

I was getting pretty good at positive affirmation, even if I didn't quite believe it myself. It was easy to get used to the idea of Sue being sick forever and never getting better. It was certainly one way to cope, at least that is what I kept telling myself.

Sue didn't say another word. She lay quietly in my lap until my leg fell asleep and I encouraged her to come down to the kitchen with me to scavenge for some chocolate. Three steps behind me, she quietly sang "*I Wish I Was a Girl*" by Counting Crows. She swayed and moved like a balloon. This is the image I keep of Sue when I think of her. Lost and stuck, all in the same the breath.

***

Sue ended up spending her entire sophomore year of college at our house. Her condition slowly got better, but not before she worked her way through a series of prescription cocktails.

She became a regular at the cardiologist office and eventually she started getting up and getting dressed every morning. We even went shopping for new clothes a few times.

Sometime in January, Sue got a part-time job filing paperwork and printing scripts for the local TV station. It was a small thing, but we were grateful at how it seemed to lift her spirits.

Watching Sue put everything on hold to fight for her life was nothing short of inspiring. She and I became closer than ever and we often talked about where we would be when it was all over.

Sue seldom talked about dying or not having enough time to do what she wanted. It was amazing to hear her speak so matter-of-factly about returning to school and becoming a newscaster. She wasn't going to let her heart stop her from following her dreams.

It was during this time I decided where my own life was heading as well. I spent countless hours sitting in Sue's darkened room in the middle of the night telling her all about how I wanted to join the Marines.

I wanted to become a strong woman our parents could look up to.

Sometimes it was easy to feel like I was living in Sue's shadow, but it wasn't her fault. She was the type of person that stood out. She was always a kind sister though.

Sue never once told me joining the Marines was stupid, never once asked me why I wanted to do it. She would simply stroke my hair in the dark and tell me what a great soldier I would be and how proud she would be of me. Sometimes in the dark, I would cry as she pulled her fingers through my hair.

Sue was what I wanted to be, what I had been trying to be my whole life.

Eventually she did go back to school. I worked even harder in my studies, planning to immediately enlist in the Marines after graduation. The day I signed my enlistment papers, my only hesitation was the fact there was a small chance I would never see Sue alive again. I told Sue about this fear after I returned from my first tour of Iraq in the wake of the attacks on September 11th.

"What if something happens to you while I am gone?" I told her one night.

"What do you mean? We're not going to put our lives on hold because you are traipsing around on a battlefield somewhere."

"That's not what I mean. I mean, what if, what if your heart..."

"Oh, shut up."

69

I could feel the tears gathering in the corners of my eyes.

"You know, you really are the best sister a girl could ask for. Always worried about me, and all. But quit it. Besides, soldiers don't cry. You big baby." Then she pulled me into a hug and held onto me until our mom called us down for dinner.

I traveled the world over four different deployments before I came home again. Finally, I settled down enough to go back to school.

I made sure she was the last person I saw before I reported for duty, each and every time. She would spend the night with me, stroking my hair in the dark like she always used to. She would be in varying stages of fatigue, but she was still my sister. I loved her and she made sure I knew she loved me back, no matter what.

Sometimes, in the middle of the night, I would wake up with the feeling Sue wasn't sick anymore. I thought maybe a miracle had occurred and I didn't have to worry about losing my sister. But the feeling would only last until I would turn my head or run my toes across the covers. Then reality would set in and I would lie awake, fighting off my soldier tears.

It would be awful of me to say Sue getting sick was the best thing to ever have happened to me, and I wouldn't say that. But it's hard to trade the way our relationship grew during those early years of her condition. For that, and that alone, I am grateful.

CHAPTER FOUR
Ethan 2001

The greatest night of my life and, quite possibly, the worst night of my life happened to be on the same day. The spring air invaded the insides of houses and worked its way through the open windows of the car. It was the type of weather strangers comment on as you wander the grocery store. It was the type of weather people say would be perfect to have all year.

I drove my father's maroon 1970 MGB with the top down that day. It had rained all afternoon and it made the fading paint job of the tiny convertible seem brand new. I was heading to Josh Powell's house. It was spring break and a bunch of my old high school friends were catching up there. Most of us had come home for the holiday. I didn't really run in the type of crowd who went on some wild vacation for spring break.

In truth I wasn't looking forward to the party as much as you would think. The old crew would all mostly be there and being away at college for the past two years had kind of made me feel like an outcast. They always say that you make your 'forever friends' in college and I could already feel my high school buddies slipping away.

I probably only got a sympathy invite from Grant. He and I had a bit of a falling out when I got accepted to State and he didn't. We were starting to recover from it and he was looking forward to catching up. I was too, but hardly at the expense of hanging out with Rachel, Ann, and Kim. All girls I thought I was in love with at one point or another. All of whom, to their credit, let me down gently, but let me down, none-the-less.

A different guy would have moved on and found a new group to hang out with, but I was a glutton for punishment. So here I was pulling into the driveway of Josh's house. By the number of cars, most everyone was already there. I parked behind Grant's faded gold Buick Seville. It was a miracle the thing still ran. He had gotten it when he turned sixteen and he spent many weekends keeping it running.

I figured everyone was expecting me by now, so I didn't bother knocking. When I got to the front door, I turned the knob and walked in. A few feet past the entry way I could see a crowd of girls hanging out in the kitchen. They were all circled around a bowl of chips and salsa. Likely Josh had made the salsa; it was his specialty.

I stood in the doorway for a moment, waiting to be noticed. When no one did, I decided rather than burst into the kitchen and announce myself, I would head to the bathroom and find my nerve. I ducked down the hallway leading to the master bedroom. When I reached the door, Grant came bursting through it.

"Ethan! What's up?" He pulled me in for a hug, and pushed me away just as fast to maintain his masculinity. "I wouldn't go in there. I destroyed that place! It wasn't pretty. Might give it ten or fifteen minutes."

"Dude, what is with you and taking dumps in other people's houses?" I said.

"When nature calls, I have to answer." He grinned. "So did Josh tell you?"

"Tell me what?"

"He invited Sue over and he's pretty sure she's on her way."

"Oh. That's cool. I didn't know they still talked. That's weird right?" I said.

"I don't know. I can't keep up anymore. Come on, you've got to see what Rachel is wearing. She looks smoking hot!"

I turned and followed Grant into the kitchen. A raucous group packed themselves around the island in the middle of the room. There was Josh and his girlfriend Jaime standing among several bottles of alcohol, all in various stages of use. They were mixing vodka with one of the many varieties of juice and soda on the counter near the stove.

Huddled around the chip bowl, drinks already in hand, were Rachel, Ann, and Kim. Then there was Heather. She was leaning against the kitchen sink recounting an article she read where drinking bottled water was the worst thing to do. Tap water, she said, was perfectly acceptable. She sipped a large glass of white wine.

When I made my way to the middle of the circle, it felt like the prodigal son had returned. Everyone shouted a hearty hello all at the same time. Their smiles showed their annoying white teeth. Yet everyone's faces lit up as I made a self-deprecating wave around the room. I moved quickly towards the counter to make myself a whiskey.

I would like to think everyone there genuinely missed me even though, since leaving for college, I hadn't heard a peep from any of them. Grant and Heather did make an effort for a while.

Heather was tall and blonde. She was by far the most mature of the group. While the rest of the girls were active in sports or music, Heather cared about the environment and political issues. She was our resident activist.

She had a knack for not coming across as a cartoon hippie. In fact, we all found it difficult to make fun of her when she cared about this issue or that. She was convincing and intelligent, so we all respected her and valued her.

Heather and I would talk on the phone once in a great while at school, but our conversations never turned romantic. She truly enjoyed my insights and I trusted her with my insecurities. She was leaving for England at the end of the summer and I was planning on quietly missing her.

Heather gave me a light punch on the arm, which was her way of saying that she was amazed I showed up. Josh came up from behind me and lifted me up in the air in a bear hug. He was a solid guy and a good friend. All the girls secretly pined away for him. His wavy brown hair and chiseled face was enough to make me write sad depressing poetry in high school.

I was constantly overlooked in favor of him in high school. He was brave enough to wear a Nike tank top in March. He probably spent the afternoon at the gym or ran in a marathon. I envied him, but tried not to let him see it. He considered me a friend and, as odd as that was, I was willing to accept it.

Josh's girlfriend, Jaime, was gorgeous. All of the girls he hung around were. But she bested the lot. She was wearing a skintight cotton dress...to a house party. Only girls that knew they were hot bothered to dress like that in such a situation.

In fact, all the girls at his house that night were attractive. I would have killed to be dating any of them, yet there I was, outnumbered five girls to every three guys but was never able to close on any of them. This was enough to make for an agonizingly depressing night.

I stood with my back against the fridge, determined not to give all my attention to one person. I looked at my watch. I was ready to go home already. The sun hadn't even gone down and things were about to get far more interesting at the Powell house.

After twenty minutes or so we moved from the kitchen into the living room. Josh turned on the stereo and we sat around swapping stories of college. The girls were telling us about the various guys they were stringing along.

I didn't contribute much to the conversation, though I would crack a joke to segue one story into someone else's. Between that and Heather graciously continuing to fill my cup with whiskey and coke, I wasn't complaining much.

The group was beginning to break apart. A few of the girls headed to the back yard to prove they could still do cartwheels, when the doorbell rang. I got up to answer it. I pulled the heavy oak door open and only darkness greeted me. The sun had set faster than I anticipated and I hit the switch to my right, flooding the porch with brightness.

Sue Anderson stood timidly in the light. We looked each other in the eye and I smiled first.

"Grant said you might grace us with your presence," I said.

"Well I didn't want you to get all the attention." She reached in for a hug. She smelled like lilac.

"Come on in," I said as we pulled apart, "Josh and everyone are in the back. Drinks in the kitchen." I moved to the side to let her in.

"Alright then," she said.

As she passed me, I took another pull of her flowery scent. It was sweet enough that I followed her to the kitchen to find another drink. She breezed right through the room and headed directly outside.

After she disappeared, I poured another whiskey and decided to head up to Josh's room to find some more CDs to listen to.

His room was in the attic, at the back end of the house. Even though Josh was still living at home and going to school in town, his room was surprisingly clean. His computer desk had a few neatly stacked piles of paper, and he had no laundry strewn about. He did have a large walk-in closet in the far corner and I suspected that it was the least organized area in the room.

I threw myself on the perfectly made bed and stared up at the ceiling for a while. I could feel the alcohol swimming in my head. There was giggling coming from the backyard below. Without me, the party was doing fine. Maybe I could stay up in his room awhile and then slip out the front door and head home without being noticed.

I decided leaving without saying goodbye would end up being more trouble than it was worth, so I sat up and turned on a lamp. I got out of bed and started rummaging through Josh's music collection sitting under his stereo by the window. He had a wide range of tastes, which was a bit surprising if you didn't really know him. He came across like a jock who'd only listen to heavy metal and rock, but his stacks of CDs had a bit of everything. From R&B to Folk Rock, there was something for everyone. Not to mention Josh had everything in alphabetical order. I was wondering if he was OCD when I heard voices coming down the hall towards the room.

I tossed the handful of CDs in my hand onto the desk and dove into the closet. I'm not sure why I hid. Maybe I still considered ducking out of the house at some point. Maybe I didn't want to remind anyone I was still there. Or maybe I was tired of talking. It was nice to see the old gang, but I was feeling just as out of place as I used to.

As I stood motionless in the closet, I heard Josh say something.

"We can talk in here okay? Is everything alright?" Josh entered the room and turned back towards the door. He evidently didn't notice that his lamp was on and sat down on his bed as Sue followed him into the room.

"It's really good to see you, Josh. Thanks for inviting me. I'm sorry I haven't called more." It was Sue's voice.

"No big deal. So what did you want to talk about?" Josh glanced at the door to his room, as if he was waiting for someone to come looking for him. Probably his girlfriend Jamie. She likely wouldn't be okay with him running off to have a secret conversation with his ex. Especially one who meant so much to him once.

Sue didn't answer right away, she moved to sit on the bed. She was so close Josh found himself scooting back a bit to give them more of a buffer. She took a deep breath. I got the distinct impression she only came over to Josh's house for this conversation.

From my vantage point in the closet, I couldn't hear as well as I would have liked. I looked around the closet for something to help me. It was, as I suspected, filled with junk. Piles of unorganized clothes and books. I was satisfied to see Josh wasn't completely perfect. When I couldn't find anything to hear with, I settled on leaning as close to the crack in the door as my body would allow. I needed to know how this was going to go down.

"Josh, I've had a lot of time to think lately. And I've been thinking about things I shouldn't."

"Like what?" Josh asked, though I got the impression from the tone of his voice he knew what she was about to say.

"I have been thinking about us a lot. We were really good together and I've missed you. I have tried to push my feelings aside, but sorta feel like we are missing out on something here."

"Sue, you were home all last year and I never heard from you. Ann told me when you came home. Where were you then?"

"I had a lot going on, Josh. I needed you, I just didn't realize it then."

"Well, I don't know what to tell you. You mean a lot to me, but I'm not in that place anymore. I have Jamie and have a new life. We're talking about enrolling at Michigan State next year. I can't stay here forever."

Sue mumbled something that I couldn't quite make out. I took my chances and pushed the door open slightly so I could see better. Sue had her head in her hands. I couldn't decide if she was crying or not. Josh didn't try to comfort her. He sat patiently, waiting.

"Listen Sue, I'll never forget what we had, but it wasn't meant to be," he said.

I was impressed. Josh certainly knew how to serve a break-up line without coming across like a complete jerk. After a moment, he stood up and put his hand on Sue's shoulder. I think I heard him mutter 'I'm sorry' but I couldn't be sure.

Sue leapt up and wrapped her arms around him. He didn't fight her off. He squeezed her tight for a few seconds and then firmly sat her back on the bed.

"I better get back downstairs," he said.

"Josh, I'm sorry..." Sue trailed off. Josh nodded and left the room. At this point I wasn't sure what to do. I was stuck in the closet until she decided to leave. I panicked a bit at the prospect of Heather coming to look for me, only to find me awkwardly spying on Sue.

Out of the blue Sue let out an audible sneeze. It caught me off guard and I took a few steps back into the closet. When I did I bumped into a bucket full of baseball bats, which promptly fell over making a loud crash. In a panic I turned and fell over the pile of bats. When the noise stopped, I froze.

"Hey?" Sue called out towards the closet, her voice straining. "Who's in there?"

I considered whether I should duck further back into the closet, but before I could make a move, the door flew open and the light from the lamp flooded in.

Sue saw me lying on the floor in a mess of sporting goods and folded her arms.

"Were you in here the whole time?"

She looked quite embarrassed.

The light from the lamp cast Sue in silhouette. Her body swayed from side to side. I put my hand over my eyes in an attempt to get a better look at her. I sighed when I couldn't see her face.

Instead of screaming or running away, Sue simply climbed into the closet with me and shut the door behind her. She made her way through the dark, knocking over things. After reaching the back of the closet, she bumped into my legs and sat down next to me. I sat up until our shoulders were touching.

"I don't think I can go back out there, Ethan," she said. I couldn't see her in the darkness, but I could feel her arm gently resting against mine. She was breathing heavily. I shifted in my seat, pushing a few fallen bats aside.

"You don't need him in order to be to be happy," I said. The blackness made it easy to speak candidly. I didn't have to worry about her face contorting or her nose wrinkling at my honesty.

"Thanks," she said.

I slowly leaned on her, assuring her that I wasn't telling her what she wanted to hear. "I mean it, Josh is a decent guy, but don't let him define your future. You're amazing all by yourself."

"Stop, okay. I think I'm blushing."

"Don't worry, I can't tell from here." We sat for a minute listening to each other breathe.

"Should we get out of here?" I asked.

"It's nice in here, quiet. Let's sit for a minute, okay?" She rested her hand on my thigh. It sent chills down my spine. Once she realized it was my leg, she moved her hand away quickly.

"So what happened? Why'd you quit school?" I said.

"Is that what everyone thinks? I didn't quit."

"So what happened then?"

"I assumed that Ann told you guys. I had to take some time off. It wasn't entirely my idea."

"Did you kill someone? It's always the quiet ones, isn't it? Am I safe in here?" I made an exaggerated gasp.

"What if I did?" She said in a chilling voice. I chuckled nervously.

"You don't have to tell me if you don't want to," I said.

"I'm sick of talking about it, okay? Can't we talk about something else? How are things with you? It's been ages."

As curious as I was to find out why the valedictorian took a year off from school, I was just as happy to be sitting alone in a dark closet with her. I had dreamed of a situation like that since I was in seventh grade. Sue and I had lived on the same street for our entire lives and this, at least to me, was the defining moment of our relationship with one another. I wasn't about to let this slip away.

"I'm doing great. Really." I lied. College wasn't exactly as I had pictured it. Of course I had delusions of grandeur before I got there. I imagined the perfect scenario where I fell in love, got top grades and was wildly popular. I may have set the bar a little high.

"That is all I get? Ethan, you're going to have to do better than that." She leaned in so close I could feel her breath across my face.

"Sue, how do you think things are going for me? I mean, you know how I am. Ever the introvert. I mean I'm really trying to put myself out there and reinvent myself, but I'm falling flat on my face mostly."

"I think you sell yourself short. I know you. You're super funny and creative. All you have to do is find the right thing to fight for."

"Fight, yeah that isn't really my strong suit, is it?" I started to slide away from her. I wanted to shrink back into the darkness. But before I could, Sue grabbed my leg and pulled me back towards her.

"Some things are worth fighting for," she whispered. "Even when you're tired and exhausted and want to give up. You still need to fight for them."

I couldn't be certain if she was talking about me or about her, but all the same, I moved back towards her. Before I knew it, I felt her hand in mine, our fingers entwined. We sat there silently, me plotting my next move, Sue likely waiting for that move.

It wasn't entirely out of the question that Sue and I should be together. I had longed for a shot with her as long as I could remember and she always seemed only an arm's length away. Maybe it was my inaction preventing it all along. Maybe Josh was just a placeholder for what she really wanted. I needed to hurry up and kiss her before the moment passed.

So I did. It was one of the smarter decisions I ever made. I thrust my face in her general direction, having nothing to guide me but my wits and even those were waning. Our noses met first. She must have been waiting for me because she was facing me, though she was looking down slightly. Our noses pressed together, I felt the insane urge to talk.

"Is this okay? Wake me up anytime," I said.

Instead of answering, she raised her head level to me and pressed her lips hard against mine. I pushed back and after the shock had set in, I opened my mouth slightly and she let out a slight whimper. It was enough to send me over the edge. I turned my whole body towards her and kissed her harder. I wasn't going to let this moment pass without making my intentions known to her. It seemed so clear to me in that moment. I loved Sue Anderson and I finally had my chance to let it be known.

As we kissed, I considered how far to take it. Should I tug at her shirt? Maybe kiss her neck and see where that took us? It was about this time that I started to think of the real reason she came to the house that night. She didn't come to find me hiding in the closet. She came for Josh.

I pulled back slightly, holding her lips a touch away from mine. She fought to kiss me again, I held her at bay, considering my next move.

"Ethan..." she moaned, almost out of breath.

"You came here for Josh," I said solemnly. I worried it might have come across as me protecting my friend's honor. In reality, I wanted to make it clear that she needed to focus on me if we were going to move forward.

It was like I had poured water over an advancing tiger. She recoiled, in a way. It was not quite disgust for my words, but rather the pain of realization. She did come for Josh, and perhaps she regretted that?

"I'm sick," she said.

"What?"

"I am sick. That's why I had to leave school. I came home and spent most of last year in and out of doctor's offices trying to get it under control."

I slumped back against a pile of clothes.

"My heart's too weak to take care of itself properly and it's larger than it should be. They're controlling it with medicine, but it's no guarantee I won't go into cardiac arrest at a moment's notice." Her voice trembled as she explained.

The sheer honesty of her words moved me. "Stop me at anytime, but how long do you have?"

"I don't know. Could be a month, could be 10 years, it really depends on a lot of factors. There are surgeries and other options available, but they tell me that I will never be completely free of it."

"I...I didn't know." I wasn't really sure what to say.

"That isn't why I kissed you Ethan. I promise. And it wasn't because of Josh either."

"Okay." I didn't want to say something insensitive and my heart was starting to hurt at the prospect of a life without Sue Anderson.

"You deserved it. Don't think I haven't noticed the way you look at me. The way you have always looked at me," she said.

"This is going to sound stupid, but I have had dreams of a moment like this. Not you being sick, but kissing you, being with you. It was nice. I don't want it to stop."

"I liked it too."

"So what does this mean?"

"I don't know," she laughed slightly, "I'm probably going to go back to school on Monday and so will you."

"And this will mean nothing?"

"I never said that. It happened, it's out there in the universe. We'll always have it. I'll fall asleep tonight thinking about it." I imagined her smiling in the dark at the notion.

She stood up and I followed her lead. I would have practically followed her to the end of the earth like a loyal horse or a trustworthy sidekick in that moment.

She pushed open the closet door. The little lamp by the bed was like a spotlight, infiltrating my eyes. I covered my face for a moment, trying hard to normalize my vision so I could finally look at her.

When I did, she forced a smile and reached around me for a big inviting hug. The kind of hug Grant gave me when my dad died. I couldn't let go.

Sue whispered in my ear as we embraced, "I'm going to be fine. I'm fighting. You should too."

She pulled away and started to walk out of the room. But then she paused, as something caught her eye. She turned, reached down onto the desk and plucked a CD case from the pile I had tossed as I scrambled into the closet.

"This is my Tom Petty CD!" She exclaimed, "I let Josh borrow it and never got it back."

"Seems like a good time to reclaim it?"

"Indeed it does." She held the CD up in the air like a trophy. The smile on her face was unbeatable. She was beautiful. Her blonde hair slightly disheveled, the tips holding the evidence of a darker dye long forgotten. She didn't look sick. She looked happy.

Sue carefully tucked the CD under her arm and released a large sigh. Then she made her way towards me and planted a pleasant kiss on my cheek.

"Thanks for being in that closet. It was the most fun I've had in a long time." she said as she turned and marched out the door.

I followed her out of the room and down into the living room. The other girls had returned from the

IAN CAHILL

backyard and were sitting in a circle, barefoot, in the middle of the room. The guys were lingering in the kitchen, mixing fresh drinks for everyone. I saw Josh nervously spot Sue and look away.

Over the bouncing power chords of *Surf Wax America*, Sue shouted to the kitchen, holding Tom Petty's Wildflowers in front of her face, "Josh, this is my CD. I'm taking it to its rightful home."

Josh was speechless for a moment as Grant laughed, then said, "It's all yours. Thanks for the good times, Tom." The boys all raised their glasses in tribute to the CD. I stood proud in the corner of the room.

Sue made a large overarching wave across the circle of girls on the floor and said, "I'm out of here." Rachel started to climb up to give Sue a hug, with Ann close behind her. But before they could reach her, Sue turned and headed down the hall and out the door. I stood there for a moment until I heard the front door shut.

The rest of the party turned back to what they were doing, and I headed for the front door. When I caught up to Sue, she was already in her car, hurriedly sticking her reclaimed CD into the stereo.

"Sue, I love you," I called to her. There was fight in me after all.

"You really mean that, don't you? Don't ever let anyone take that from you." It was a bit condescending, but in the moment I couldn't see the forest for the trees.

"Can I call you?" I said.

"Definitely," she said. And with that she started up the engine of her shiny silver Honda Civic. It took a minute, but eventually Tom Petty's soft guitar echoed throughout the driveway. Sue turned it up and slammed the car into gear. I backed up slightly as she pulled her car out into the street.

She offered me a small wave and sang a few bars of the song before driving away. I could hear her singing as she turned the corner and headed out of the neighborhood.

On Monday I went back to school, thinking of nothing else but Sue's soft lips. I did call her; I could barely wait more than a day. And when I did, we talked for hours. She told me her strength had been coming back and she was excited to be back in school full-time. We often talked about seeing each other when we were home, or planning a trip over the summer, just the two of us.

Eventually though, the phone calls became fewer and fewer. Then they stopped entirely. Before I knew it, we had graduated from college. I moved to Denver and took a marketing job with a micro-brewery. Sue had moved to Boston. There she was, climbing the bottom rung of the local news ladder.

I managed to keep up to date on all things Sue through Ann for the next couple of years. Ann seemed to be the only person, besides Sue's parents, who spoke to her on a regular basis. But that wasn't ideal and eventually the distance got the better of us.

Before I knew it, I was married with a kid on the way. Sue was simply a beautiful memory that I clung to on the days when I felt lonely or sentimental. She was the one that got away. I know that now. Whether she knows it or not, I guess that's for her to decide.

At least once every six months or so, I have the urge to google her name or try to contact Ann to see what she knows. I never go through with it, though. Sue has become like a band I used to like. The first album is so amazing you wear it out listening to it. Sure, the band has newer albums out, but you love the first one so much that you don't want to clutter your brain or risk tainting those songs with any others. Nothing exists outside of that one perfect record. Sue has a new life now and I'm not a part of it. And maybe it's better to not know anything about it, lest it sully that terribly amazing night in Josh's closet.

CHAPTER FIVE
Catherine 2005

Asparagus. I had shared an apartment with Sue Anderson for over a year and the thing that sticks out the most is the asparagus. We could run out of milk, have no bread, no trash bags, no sugar, but you could always count on a steamed side of asparagus for supper at night.

Sue was never on a diet, but she always tried to eat healthy in her condition, plus she loved those little green sticks. It had its own special smell that seemed to get in my clothes and hair as she tirelessly prepared it in the next room.

When I would join her for dinner at our plastic-coated brown and green breakfast table from the vintage shop down the street, there they were. Like sandbags protecting the pork chops from the imminent danger of a massive wave of mashed potatoes.

Those thin stalks never looked greener or tastier on any TV show or magazine cover. She had it down to a science. They were idyllic, if asparagus was even allowed to be. And yet, time and time again, we sat in silence and ate the perfectly prepared greens. There was always a distance to her. Her head was in a space that I would never understand. She was almost robotic as she snapped into her asparagus.

I half expected her skin to turn green instead of the smooth bronze glow that peaked out from underneath her ancient Guns N' Roses t-shirt. When there was leftover asparagus, as there inevitably would be, she dutifully packed a bundle into her lunch bag to take to work the next day.

Sue was dealing with a lot of heavy shit during this time, so I guess I don't blame her for keeping to herself. We hadn't even planned on being roommates. It just happened. We looked at the same gorgeous apartment on the exact same day at the exact same time. The landlord didn't really care who got it. I was prepared to fight, but I never got the chance. She asked me to coffee to sort it out and I went. Mainly because I thought she was cute, but still figured she would try to talk me out of the place.

Instead, we became roommates. It was simply a solution to our problem. The place was amazing, the rent was affordable and there was plenty of space for both of us.

Sue didn't even give me her sob story about being sick. She saved that for the first time the dishwasher needed to be unloaded. She was pretty care-free and I trusted her immediately. She usually worked crazy hours, so she was seldom home anyhow.

I was toiling away as a waitress at a bar & grill called Davenport's. It wasn't exactly my dream scenario, but it put food on the table. I longed for something better and Sue seemed like the type of person to encourage me to go out and make something of myself.

She worked for a small TV station outside of Boston, where she wrote stories for the local news. Occasionally on the weekends, I would see her in front of the camera covering random personal interest stories. She loved it and it filled my heart to listen to her talk about it.

Her drive, even considering she was often wiped out and exhausted at the end of each day, was part of the reason why I wanted her to stay my roommate.

One weekend, her friend Ann came to visit. Ann was a singer in a band called The Spotless and was in town for a few gigs. Sue offered to let her stay at our place while the rest of the band holed up in a cheap motel nearby.

I didn't object, I wanted to see what a friend of Sue's was like. I hadn't gotten to see that side of her before.

Ann arrived on a Friday night, after her show was over. I wasn't sure what time it was when the banging started on the door, but it felt late, which is saying something considering what a bar rat I was.

Sue had only been home from the station for a few minutes and was fumbling around in the kitchen. I'd heard her come in and was attempting to fall back asleep when Ann stumbled through the front door.

"Sue, oh my God, you look amazing. It's one a.m. and I could eat you up!"

"You haven't even been here 30 seconds and you are lying to me already," Sue said.

I sat up in bed and reached for a t-shirt.

"Is your roommate home?" I heard Ann say from the other room.

"Yeah, I think she's asleep, though I'm sure your drunk ass woke her up."

Given that I was already awake, I went to the living room to meet our guest. As I entered the room, both of them looked towards my sleepy eyes. I smiled and offered a casual wave.

"Hey. I'm Catherine...Cat." I reached for Ann's hand. She smelled like a bar, but her wavy black hair framed her face just right. She had been doused in glitter that I was sure would be everywhere. As she shook my hand, her long, bright-white fingernails felt cold on my wrist. I tried to act cool, but she was definitely making my bottom tingle.

"Sorry I woke you up. Shitty manners," Ann said.

"Don't worry about it, I'm used to Sue getting in late."

"Oh really, Sue! You slut, you."

"You wish. Most nights, I don't leave the station until midnight or one," Sue said matter-of-factly.

Her job was a badge of honor, and when she spoke of it, it was never with disdain.

"Well since you're both up, who's making drinks?" Ann said with a smile.

I knew Sue wasn't one to drink much, since it may or may not interfere with her myopathy, but she was open to a glass of wine on occasion.

I wasn't completely thrilled at the idea of living with someone that could drop dead at any moment. At least...this is how I interpreted it when she first told me. I mean, she didn't look sick and assured me that she was doing everything in her power to keep her condition under control.

And she did. It wasn't just the asparagus. She was committed to this crazy routine—medicine, exercise, eating right. When she did have free time it was usually spent poring over medical studies and internet forums, trying to learn as much as she could about new and experimental treatments for her condition.

And don't think I didn't try to get her out of the house.

Sure, I had friends of my own, but I always tried to include her. Living with someone, sharing personal space, is a very intimate thing. So I wanted her to feel like family. But she rarely accepted my invites.

It only took a few weeks before I didn't even think about her heart. She never wanted me to feel sorry for her, so I think she downplayed it whenever she could. And aside from the occasional weekend spent on the couch watching episodes of Dirty Jobs, she was perfectly normal.

I went into the kitchen and twisted the cap off a cheap bottle of red wine. I poured two embarrassingly large glasses and one modest sized one for Sue. We all laughed at the runt of a glass when I handed it to Sue and moved to the living room. Sue warmed up some leftover split-pea soup as Ann and I tackled our vats of wine.

"So Ann, what's it like being in a band? Do guys hit on you constantly?" I said, trying to feel her out.

"Well, not really. I mean, yes they do, but I'm pretty protected when I want to be. I go straight from the dressing room to the stage, or to our shitty RV. So I don't mingle unless I want to," Ann said.

"So where to next?" Sue asked between slurps of soup.

"Well, I wanted to talk to you about that, actually..." Ann said before taking a huge gulp of wine. "What would you two think of me hanging around here for a while? The tour is over after Boston and we haven't really planned the next thing. I mean, it wouldn't be for that long. The album is finished and we'll mix it and send it out to labels. I'll be out of your hair before you know it."

I didn't say anything. I wanted to see what Sue had to say first. I wanted Ann to stay; she was a breath of fresh air and very easy to look at. I looked to Sue for her reaction.

"Well, I suppose staying here beats getting a real job," Sue said.

Ann started to argue, but Sue held up her finger to prevent her from saying anything.

"I sleep on the right side and you can't have sex in my bed."

Ann didn't need to say anything. She just gave a giant squeal and wrapped Sue in a bear hug. "I love, love, love you!"

"Ahem..." I started. Ann came over and gave me a gentle hug as well.

"And you too, Cat. I hope this is okay?" She winked and returned to her wine glass, which was nearly empty.

***

Ann ended up staying a lot longer than any of us had imagined. At first she had offered to pay rent, to which Sue and I said no. Ann protested, so we settled on her buying groceries occasionally. Before we knew it, Ann had been there for a month.

We had gotten so used to her being around, she became incorporated into both our routines. I'll forever be grateful she stayed with us for two reasons. The first reason was simple: I fell in love with her. I never actually told her this, but she knew how I felt.

I never was great at explaining my sexuality to anyone. Even when I was a little girl, I knew that it was never going to be boys, but I didn't know exactly how to say it.

As a result, it always took me unbearable amounts of time to even get the courage to ask a girl if they were gay. I still wasn't sure about Ann, but seeing her day in and day out at the apartment drove me crazy. I knew, at some point, I would have to bring it up.

Sue was gone most evenings, which gave Ann and I a lot of time to get to know one another. The nights with only the two of us were amazing. Ann and I talked about everything under the sun. For me, this was the relationship I had been waiting a lifetime for. It sounds stupid, but I started to treat Ann like my girlfriend, whether she realized it or not.

Ann was quite flippant about the details of her life, but I got the feeling she was often sincere when she was trying not to be. These conversations were eye-opening, often making my life as a waitress seem putrid and lowly. Listening to Ann talk about life on the road with her band put me in a different world. I often found myself ready to pack up and live the rest of my life on the road like Christopher McCandless.

Ann said things like, "I spent the night in Albuquerque once on the floor of a mobile home. The entire night the guys watched porn and videos of soccer hooligans rioting. I tried to play it cool, but I was the only girl there and was freaking out."

Ann was so comfortable in her skin she didn't think twice about snuggling with me on the couch or passing naked through the living room. I tried to play it cool and not be the cliché lesbian ogling my sexy roommate, but frankly it was hard sometimes. I got the feeling she was doing it on purpose and that made it even more appealing.

One of those nights, I will keep with me forever. It was a Friday and I had worked the day shift. Sue was supposed to meet us for dinner at this new place called

The Hollow Leg but at the last second she cancelled. There was breaking news coverage for a pending snow storm, so I called Ann to let her know I was going to head back to our place.

When I entered the apartment, Ann was standing in the doorway to the kitchen. She was in Sue's old faded Guns N' Roses t-shirt and glittered pink underwear. She had already started dinner and I could tell some of Sue's classic asparagus was working its magic on the stove.

Ann was reading an issue of *Rolling Stone* magazine with the White Stripes on the cover. The Tuesday of her days-of-the-week underpants set were slowly moving side to side in some sort of musical rhythm that I couldn't quite make out. I looked away, too embarrassed to sort out the song. She cracked a smile as I laid eyes on her, but did not look up right away.

I threw my keys into the small basket by the door and headed towards her. Again, she didn't look up and at the last second stepped aside to give me wide berth into the kitchen.

"You're making me dinner? This is impressive!" I announced. Ann didn't look up from her magazine, but the grin was still on her face. "What are we having?"

"Spiced rubbed brisket with roasted carrots and Suesparagus," Ann said.

"Really?"

"Fuck off. I'm making fish sticks, Honey. And Suesparagus," Ann said.

She called me Honey and my whole body tingled. I giggled as I peeked into the oven, where a pan of fish sticks was indeed cooking. The choice struck me as quite whimsical. Who bought fish sticks at our age? In my fervor, I leaned into Ann's face and kissed her on the cheek.

"Thank you for making dinner," I said.

"Don't mention it. Why don't you go get changed out of your stinky ass work shirt? This will be ready soon."

I looked down at my polo shirt, stained with grease and carrying a slight stench of potato. Embarrassed, I pulled at my shirt a little and mentally counted the stains.

"That's actually kind of gross, you should burn that thing." Ann said. Then she came toward me and tugged at my shirt. I let go and looked her in the eyes as she pulled it over my head, wadded it up and tossed it across the room into the trash.

There I was, left only in my flesh colored bra and black work pants. My first instinct was to fold my arms over my chest, but I resisted with all my might.

"Please, leave that thing in the trash. It's spent." Ann was shaking off her hands as if soot or green slime covered them.

She didn't seem at all concerned I was standing in front of her in my bra. It certainly was an interesting scenario considering she wasn't wearing any pants. I straightened my back and strode across the kitchen to retrieve a beer from the fridge. On my way, I swatted at Ann's ass and she let out a shrill yelp, which to me sounded like delight.

When I reached for the magnetic bottle opener stuck to the door Ann squealed, "Me, Me, Me."

I leaned back into the fridge, the cold air running across my skin, and grabbed a second beer for her.

I popped the tops and carried them into the living room. Ann toddled behind me like a lost puppy. My insides were all a flutter now. I wasn't sure I was going to be able to keep my cool.

I set one of the beers down on the coffee table and took a swig off the one I still had. Ann scooped up the other and took a long draw from it.

"That's really cold!" She touched the cold bottle to my neck, I instantly clammed up and shrieked. I'll admit, sometimes it was fun to play the downy innocent, especially when trying to entice a fox like Ann. I still was waiting for the inevitable let down where she would tell me she wasn't gay and she really liked me, and all, but it was never going to happen. But I figured I owed it to myself to play it out a bit first.

Ann plopped down on the sofa and tossed a few throw pillows onto the frazzled green armchair in the corner. Then she pulled open the tiny little drawer inside of the coffee table and came out with a small bag of pot.

"Listen, I know you're fit and all, but wanna get high with me?" Ann's eyelashes fluttered.

"Well, how can I say no to that face?" I smiled and took another pull of my beer.

Ann then patted on the couch next to her, beck-oning me to join her. I took yet another drink of my beer and found the bottom. I timidly sidled up to her, touching her thigh with mine. I watched as she care-fully spread out her supplies and gently rolled a joint from a small pack of zig-zags and a modest amount of pot.

I salivated as I watched her lick the paper to seal the edges. With my knees pressed together, I cleared my throat and Ann's eyes met mine.

"Cat, you've smoked before right?"

"Well, yeah, but I'd already been drunk both times, so I'm not really sure what it's actually like. You might have to keep an eye on me."

"It'll be fine, let it be. I write my best songs high, sometimes I think I should get stoned way more."

"Does Sue know you smoke?"

"I think so. She isn't one to judge, but I don't think she would let herself enjoy it if she did it, so I've never asked her to."

"I worry about her sometimes," I said.

"Me too. I love her so much; she doesn't deserve the hand that was dealt to her."

"Yeah, sometimes I think she purposely over-works herself to prove she's better than her heart prob-lems."

"Get on her for that! I couldn't stand it if some-thing happened to her."

Ann's words trailed off for a moment and in the gap of silence that filled it, she tucked the joint between her gorgeous soft lips and lit the end. A few puffs later, the end was bright red and smoldering.

Then she passed it to me. I put it to my mouth, letting it sit there as Ann handed me the lighter. I relit the end and took a slow breath in. When I did this, Ann leaned into my face and began to massage my earlobe between her thumb and forefinger. The mixture of the smoke and her touch forced my eyes closed. Holy shit, was this happening?

We passed the joint back and forth three or four times before I lost count. Ann had slumped down into the couch, her bare legs caressing mine when she moved to pass the joint. My whole body was tense. I was hoping the weed would loosen me up enough to ask Ann if she ever considered being with a girl, but it hadn't yet.

Without thinking, I turned my head and focused on a print Sue had hung on the wall. It was a portrait by Caravaggio; I think she called it *Sick Bacchus*. It always creeped me out. I knew it had some symbolic meaning to Sue about her condition, but in my current state all I could do was stare into his eyes.

As I stared, I could feel Ann shuffling next to me, without thinking I moved my hand over her thigh to make her still. My hand met hers and before I knew it, Ann had straddled me and was kissing my neck and shoulder. It happened so fast I didn't have time to think about what it meant. I pulled her face to mine and we kissed hard.

I stroked the bare skin of her legs with my hands and Ann fingered the straps of my bra as we kissed. It felt like she had been here before. She didn't make any attempt to take off her shirt or remove anything from my body, but continued to kiss me furiously. She didn't weigh a lot but she still managed, eventually, to make my legs fall asleep. I shifted slightly in hopes she would sink deeper into my lap.

It was about this moment my nostrils were thick with the smell of smoke. I asked myself where the joint had ended up, but didn't dare move to look for it. I wasn't about to pass up this moment with Ann. I had been fantasizing about for weeks.

We kissed for a moment longer when the smell of burning grew stronger. This time, I wondered out loud what it could be.

"Do you smell that?" I asked. Ann pulled her face away from mine and tilted her head up to sniff the air.

"Oh shit!"

Ann leapt up and darted into the kitchen. The source of the smell was one-hundred-percent evident now. As I lay on the couch, I could see her framed between the refrigerator and the recliner. She looked somewhat defeated as she scooped the burnt mess that was the asparagus into the trashcan. Her breasts were slightly swinging back and forth under her t-shirt with each pass of the spoon.

I rested my head on the armrest of the sofa and watched her silently upside down. I was stoned. I was euphoric and half expected her hair to fall upwards towards the ceiling.

The phone rang and Ann disappeared to the other side of the kitchen to answer it. I closed my eyes for a minute and for some reason began humming *This Little Light of Mine*.

Eventually, she wandered back into the room, her face vacant and lost.

"What's up?" I asked. She said nothing at first, but then suddenly ran into the bedroom without saying a word.

"Ann," I screamed, "What's going on?"

"It's Sue," She called from the other room. That was all I needed to know. I shot up and ran into my room to pull on some clothes.

We took my car to the hospital. I have no idea how we actually got there. The snow from the storm had already started to fall and my head was pounding. It felt like my eyes were shifting back and forth all on their own. I tried with all my might to concentrate on getting there in one piece. It didn't help that Ann was hysterical in the passenger seat. I wondered if she'd ever been in a situation like this before.

Sue had gone to the doctor many times since we moved in together, but never as an emergency. If something really bad happened, I didn't even have her parents' phone number.

"Ann, was it Sue who called you?"

"Yes, she sounded really bad. How much further?"

"Well it's got to be a good sign she was the one calling and not a doctor right?"

"Yeah, that makes sense. God, where is this place? Can you hurry?"

I pressed my foot to the pedal to ease Ann's mind and then gradually slowed down again. It was all I could do to keep the car on the road in the snow. Pretty soon the hospital appeared over the hill and I turned into the parking lot.

We maneuvered past the front desk, the elevator and several winding corridors before we got to the room where Sue was. I was grateful that Ann did most of the talking to get us there. We didn't knock when we entered the room, but when Ann saw Sue, she stormed the bed and frantically kissed Sue's forehead over and over.

Sue was lying in bed, an IV secured into her hand. She looked exhausted and had a bandage covering part of her forehead. She took a long deep breath when she recognized us.

"Sue, what happened?" I said.

Sue let out a large audible sigh, "There was a table that really wanted me to dance on it. And then I blacked out. I guess I overdid it a bit." As she said this, she used her hands to recreate the scene of falling off a table.

"I thought you were at work?"

"I was. Sharon brought sangria for the long haul. We figured we would be covering the storm all night. I only had a few."

"Sue. What were you thinking?" As I finished the question, I couldn't help but feel like a hypocrite. Here I was, high as a kite, judging her. But the fact of the matter was drinking and heart disease shouldn't mix. Sue knew that, but it wasn't my place to lecture her.

"God dammit Sue. You can't do that!" Ann said raising her voice, as tears came streaming down her face.

"I wanted to feel normal for one stupid second, I'm sorry." Sue's eyes were becoming glassy. "I didn't think it was going to be a big deal."

A tall, older man in a lab coat, which was far too short for his body, came ambling in. His face was buried in a chart board. His shoes made an odd squeaky noise when he walked and he sounded like he had the sniffles.

"Which one of you is Sue Anderson?" He glanced around the room with a casual grin on his face.

"Present," Sue replied, raising her hand in the air.

"I'm Dr. Wilson. How are you feeling tonight?"

"Well you know, a bit peckish? Maybe little dizzy. Sleepy," Sue said.

"Alright dear, it looks like we're going to keep you here overnight. We want to run a few tests to see how your heart is doing. When was the last time you had a check for your myopathy?"

"It's been about three months I guess. I've be doing so good..." Sue's voice trailed off.

"Just relax and enjoy your stay. We won't bother you too much, okay? I'll be back in a while to get started." He patted her knee softly. Then he turned and left the room without so much as acknowledging Ann or me.

After a moment, when Dr. Wilson was far enough down the hall Sue smiled and said, "He smelled like bologna." Suddenly the weight of the moment lifted from the room. Ann started to laugh through her tears and I took a deep breath and sat at the foot of Sue's bed.

"I realized I don't even have your parents' phone number or anything. So you aren't allowed to do this anymore. But I'm glad you're okay," I said.

"Well I hope I am. They haven't really told me much."

"So did you fall? Or did you pass out?"

"Well I was fine for a little while, and then I started getting really dizzy and before I could tell anyone, I fell off the table."

"So how did you get here?"

"The intern drove me. I came to long enough to insist they not call an ambulance. He made sure I got inside and then I sent him back to the station. I feel fine now."

Ann sat down in the chair next to the bed and was bobbing her head back and forth, staring at our reflection in the large picture window opposite her.

"Ann? Are you drunk?" Sue asked.

"Cat and I smoked some pot before you called."

Sue looked at me surprised, "Really?"

"Yeah," I shrugged, "my head is killing me though."

This caused Sue and Ann to start laughing again. I didn't think it was funny and folded my arms in front of my chest and wrinkled up my face.

We wanted to stay all night, but Sue was adamant we go back to the apartment before the storm got any worse. We did as she said, against our will. I sucked down a bottle of water and a pack of chocolate-covered donuts as we made our way through the maze of the hospital and back to the car. It made me feel a little better as we drove back to the apartment in silence.

The door to the apartment was still unlocked. We had left in such a hurry we must have forgotten to lock it. I tossed my keys back into the basket by the door and Ann pushed past me. I thought about our make-out session as I stared at the sofa. Did it mean anything or did it only happen because she was high?

Ann disappeared into the kitchen and came back out with a handful of marshmallows. She was pulling them into her mouth with her tongue. I watched her do this as she walked towards me. Without a word she reached out and pulled me into a big hug. She squeezed me tighter than I thought she was capable of. The smell of the marshmallows in her hand wafted in the air.

"Jesus, that was scary. Thanks for being here. If I had to deal with that shit alone, I don't know what I would have done."

She held on tight for a while. We were both exhausted, so we broke apart and retreated to our rooms to pass out. I lay awake in bed, attempting to process the evening.

I kept telling myself that Sue simply drank a bit too much and fell off of a table. It could have happened to anyone. The alternative was too much to bear. This was the first time Sue showed her illness outwardly. Was this going to become the norm? Could I deal with it? It was a selfish thought.

Eventually my eyelids became too heavy and I fell asleep.

***

A month later, Sue was gone. I found myself lying upside down on the couch once more. The room left a lot to be desired. Most of the photos that once adorned the walls were hers, gone. The end tables, gone. The refrigerator magnets, the little dogs and the plastic yellow corn on the cobs, gone.

I was never terribly fond of asparagus in the first place. But after a week without Sue, I found myself in the kitchen coating them in butter, searching for a suitable pot to steam them in.

I get why she had to leave. The test results showed the walls of her heart had thinned further and she had to start a new round of meds. She became even stricter with her diet and exercise routines. Things could change for her in a split second and she felt a strong need to be close to her family.

I can't blame her for deciding to get an apartment near her parents. She worked out a plan to transfer to the TV station in her hometown, so she wasn't entirely depressed, although she told me she felt like she was taking a step backwards.

I was going to miss her. I cared about her a great deal. Maybe I wasn't as close to her as Ann was, but we had formed a bond. We both accepted each other for who we were, with no judgment.

Ann had decided to move out around the same time as Sue, so it was doubly crushing for me. Ann and I never addressed the night we kissed. I don't think she was scared or embarrassed, I just don't think she thought about it that deeply.

She left the day after Sue. She packed all her bags into her car and returned to the empty apartment with a hastily wrapped box.

"It's not much, thought you'd want it though."

Inside was a rough cut of her band's album, as well as a small bag of pot. I was about to tell her that I didn't really want the weed when she leaned in and kissed me full on the mouth. I pulled her close, and for a few seconds, we were one person, entwined in passion and trust.

She pulled away before I did. Smiling, she took a few steps towards the door before lunging back at me and giving me a tight hug. I whispered, "Thank you," in her ear and she was off. I was alone.

After Ann and Sue left, I quit my job and went back to school. I figured if Ann could be in a rock band and Sue could fight through heart disease, the least I could do was try to aim for something better. I ended up studying anthropology and working on a grant about human sexuality.

I don't eat asparagus nearly as often as I did then, but when I do, I always think back to the night that Ann and I came together to be there for Sue. It seems silly looking back on it, but it was one of those moments in your life that end up being bigger than yourself.

The three of us came together and for a short time it was beautiful.

It was hard at first, to move along with my new life while Sue tried to restart hers back home. It was always on the nights when I made asparagus I really missed having Sue around. Even though she was sick, she never made it a crutch, and I'm grateful she let me be in her life, even if she didn't really need me to be.

CHAPTER SIX
Jack 2006

Thank God for my sonic bomb alarm clock. It boomed in my ears as I stirred in bed. I pressed my palms into my eyes. It isn't normal for me to get smashed on a Tuesday, but the blond in the super tight jeans convinced me. She succeeded in separating herself from the pack of girls who followed me around the bar all night. To her credit, I let her spend the night.

The sun forced its way through the window and the alarm clock continued its incessant screaming. I shifted my weight onto my right side and pushed the off button on the alarm. I could tell I was naked and, with my eyes still closed, felt around for my underwear.

I came across the blonde, dead asleep and equally as naked next to me. I felt a tug of guilt as I tried to remember her name. It was impressive she was still asleep. I made it a point to buy the loudest alarm clock on the market for this type of situation. I supposed she could have been pretending to be asleep. That way she could avoid the awkward conversation you have to have with the stranger you slept with the night before.

That, or she was too shy to admit to herself she slept with a minor celebrity.

Either way, I didn't have time to find out. I threw the covers off of both of us, slapped her ass and headed to the bathroom. As I went, I took the slightest look at the naked specimen reaching on the ground for what I could only assume were her pants. Very impressive Jack, I thought to myself.

"I gotta get to the station, there are fruit smoothies in the fridge. Feel free to shower before you take off. You were tremendous by the way, that one thing you did with your elbow, I'm filing that one away for later!"

I pulled open the shower curtain, stole one last glance at her blushing smile, and buried myself under hot water. It was going to be a long day.

***

I pulled in the parking lot of WLLM-TV and pulled my Land Rover into the spot closest to the door. The station had graciously, under my request, put up a little sign that read 'Jack Rogers - News Anchor' in the little patch of grass in front of the parking spot. This ensured it was always free and clear for yours truly.

I slid out of the driver's seat and reached in the back for a suit. I always kept one or two in the car in case of a breaking news emergency. As I tugged on the hanger of the nearest suit jacket, I couldn't help but notice a dark blur out of the corner of my eye.

A jet-black pencil skirt stuck out of the back of a trunk across the aisle. The first thought I had was easily 'nice ass' and I lingered a moment as the skirt moved from side to side in the sunlight. This would turn out to be my first impression of Sue Anderson, which as sexist as it sounds wasn't a bad place to start.

I finally took my eyes off her butt and tried to shake off the last of my hangover. I took a big gulp of purple Gatorade and headed inside to change. The evening news was right around the corner and I needed to get dressed, styled and prepped for the top stories. The camera needed me.

I had my own office with a private bathroom. I ducked in to take a leak. The daily team meeting started while I was washing my hands, so I threw on my suit and made my way to the conference room.

Earl Pace sat at the head of the table shuffling his notes and scribbling on a small notepad the size of a lunch box sandwich. He was my executive producer and the genius who gave me my first chance in front of the camera. His five-foot-two frame shifted as I entered the room. I was late as usual.

"Afternoon, Jack." Earl purposely raised his voice. It was condescending and passive-aggressive, but I read it loud and clear.

As I nodded, I turned my attention to the coffee station in the corner of the room. I always took my coffee black. I told myself it came off as confident and a sign of strength. I never particularly cared for the flavor, but if I wanted to squash the throbbing in my forehead, I would deal with it.

The rest of the room was already full with the rest of the staff. I cradled my cup of coffee as I worked my way towards an empty seat at the large oval table in the center of the room. As I sat down, the doll in the black pencil skirt came bursting in the room.

"I'm sorry, Mr. Pace."

Earl waved her off. "Don't worry about it dear, please sit down."

A bit shaken, she took a seat and flashed a smile at me before burying her eyes into her notebook. Her hair folded up neat into a tight bun, giving off a sort of sexy librarian vibe, minus the glasses. By the way she fidgeted with her notebook, you could tell she was nervous. Yet something about the way she sat there told me she had been in a newsroom before. I doubted she was green.

"Alright, let's get started. The striking lady to my right is Sue Anderson. She's joining us from KKRN outside of Boston. Big time market, so she should be able to bring a lot to our humble table. She was associate producer there and will serve the same role here. Say hello."

The room sat quiet for a moment, we weren't quite sure if he was talking to Sue or to the rest of us. I spoke up first.

"Sue, on behalf of everyone at WLLM, welcome. I'm sure you'll fit right in around here." I gave her my patented Jack Rogers smile.

"Thank you. Jack right?"

"Absolutely." I reached my hand across the table to shake hers. She looked me up and down for a moment and eventually took my hand. Her hands were soft, she definitely used some kind of lotion.

"Let's get this over with, people. First order of business. Jack is emcee at the PPCC, Pooches for Prostate Cancer Carnival next weekend. You can't make this stuff up. I need a team there to shoot a piece and b-roll for a small spot we promised," Earl said.

Again, there was a moment of silence and the room stirred. "I'll do it," Sue's hand shot up. She immediately began looking around the room expecting others to join her.

"Diving in head first Anderson, I like it. You're a regular hot shot," I said.

Sue blushed.

"Who else?" Earl said. Greg, who normally drove the TV truck and Reilly, the intern, both half raised their hands. "Thanks to you. Moving on."

The rest of the meeting was dreadful. My head was still pounding and I spent most of the time watching Sue jot down notes and nodding my head as if I were in complete control of my faculties.

Local news in our town wasn't rocket science. Most of the time the top story stretched the boundaries of interest. Otherwise, it dealt with the local school district or town hall. Real riveting stuff.

When the meeting concluded, the team spilled out of the conference room. Sue was moving pretty fast, so I had to double step to catch her.

"Hot Shot, wait up!" I called. She turned to greet me with a deep sigh and a well-timed smirk. "I wanted to welcome you to the station again. I've got a pretty good handle on the way things work around here, so if you need anything, don't hesitate." I gestured to my office.

"Jack. Rockefeller. Rogers." She folded her arms as she spoke. "I know what you are doing, but I think I'll be fine. Not my first rodeo," she said and turned back the other direction, "and don't call me Hot Shot."

No one had called me Rockefeller since high school. How did she know that?

I wanted to call after her, but instead ducked back into my office to work on my script for the evening. After a couple of hours, I still couldn't get what she said out of my head. Did she do research on me before she came? If she did, it was impressive if not a little scary.

Sue and I had little interaction for the next week. I spent most of the time asking everyone at the station what they knew about her. And I mean everyone. I left no stone unturned. But only a few people had a chance to talk to her at any length. The dead-ends were piling up.

Meanwhile, Sue wasn't wasting any time getting up to speed. She hit the ground running, outshining even our most valued folks. She was there at all hours of the day, culling stories, making phone calls, acquainting herself with the newsroom.

She even had the nerve to reorganize the different types of printer paper in the copy room.

Who was this girl?

By the afternoon of the dog cancer carnival, I still was no closer to solving how she knew my high school nickname. I decided I would get her alone and personally interrogate her until I figured out what her angle was.

Greg, Reilly, and Sue met me at the station. Greg and Reilly drove the station's van, while Sue and I drove our own cars to the event.

I was wearing a light blue tie and a ribbon for Prostate Cancer, which I matched nicely with a camel-colored suit. It was a mild spring afternoon, the wind pulled the trees back and forth, and it looked like it might rain.

It was in my best interest to volunteer for events like this. I worked hard to become a respected member of the community. These types of events helped solidify my celebrity status in the area.

When we arrived at the church parking lot where they were holding the event, it was nothing short of an embarrassment. Using the term carnival was a joke.

I know it was for a good cause, but the parking lot looked more like a sad garage sale. There was a smattering of tents set up on the left poised to pass out cancer literature and take up donations from the crowd.

On the right was a single battered trailer that billowed smoke from its roof. The poor souls inside were preparing to serve hamburgers and hot dogs to the patrons as they arrived.

The rest of the lot was a mix of rinky-dink parlor games like ring toss and duck pond. This was nowhere near what I had pictured in my head when I agreed to host the event. All the same, this is where we found ourselves. To the credit of my team, we all plastered on giant fake smiles and got to work.

Sue took charge almost immediately. She directed me to the truck bed serving as my stage for the afternoon. I got to work on some light announcements. She sent Greg and Reilly to grab pick up shots of the carnival games for b-roll. Then she ran off to find a more detailed itinerary from the event organizers.

Greg was a little incensed Sue had bossed him around. Frankly, I was as well but things were put in motion so fast we never had a chance to complain.

And we couldn't argue with the fact the tasks Sue set forth were necessary, so we kept our mouths shut and got to work without causing conflict. Of course, before I could do anything of value, I took the time to flirt with a cute little brunette hanging out around the stage. She turned out to be the PPC President's daughter.

The clock ticked down to the start of the carnival and I took my place on stage, behind the microphone, where I was born to be. I welcomed people as they started to pour into the parking lot. I always enjoyed commanding a crowd.

"Welcome everyone to the 3rd annual Pooches for Prostate Cancer Carnival. I'm thrilled you finally came to your senses and invited me to emcee. Really, it's great to see so many dogs in the audience, and their wives. But seriously, we're here for a great cause. Whether you or someone you know and love has been affected by prostate cancer, rest assured that your presence here means a lot. Now don't let me stop you. Get out there, play some games and donate to a great cause. Donations can be made at the blue tents to your left. I'll be here all day, so come say hi!"

There was a smattering of applause as I stepped down to search for the president's daughter. Instead, I found Sue.

She sat perched on a small folding metal chair. One of the metal legs bent inward and it forced her small frame to lean forward towards the asphalt.

"Hey, Hot Shot?"

She raised her head in surprise. I guess I expected her to be crying or something based on the awkward position in which the chair forced her to sit, but when she saw me she stood up. As she did she pushed her dress down with her palms.

Under the early afternoon sun, she was pretty cute. You could tell she took care of herself. Even with the demands of the job, she had flawless make-up and hair. She didn't like me. I knew that. I wasn't really that interested in getting to know her either, but I had to find out what she knew about me.

"Rockefeller...hey, great...speech. And stop calling me Hot Shot."

"Stop calling me Rockefeller and I'll think about it. Where did you hear that anyways?"

"Oh I know everything about you Jack...everything." She stared at me so intensely I took a few steps backwards out of sheer instinct. As I did so, I stumbled over a trashcan.

I composed myself and then smirked, "I'll find out, Hot Shot. I have eyes all over town." I motioned across the parking lot for a grand effect.

She simply rolled her eyes and began consulting a stack of papers fixed onto a clipboard. Say what you want, but as she stood there with one foot wrapped around the ankle of her other leg, she looked so smart and, dare I say, sexy. I bit my lip as I watched her chest rise and fall in heavy breaths. Yeah, I was staring at her breasts. They were inviting, and I had nothing to apologize for.

Sue looked up at me and said, "I'm gonna go check and see how Greg is faring. You should probably go mingle." She flicked her hand in the opposite direction.

"You don't want to get on my bad side, Sue. It's a dark and smarmy place. Believe me, I live there."

"I'll remember that," she said with a smile. I could see in her eyes she was being playful. I was more than happy to oblige.

Slowly, she became almost bearable. In truth, I had no good reason to have ill feelings for her, at least outside of her having insider information about my checkered past. Regardless, she was damn good at her job and easy to look at. It was a win-win.

I rolled up the sleeves of my dress shirt and headed out into the crowd, hoping to find some adoring fans. Sue headed into the other direction to find the guys.

The crowd at the carnival did not exactly look the part of adoring fans, so I had to look a little harder than normal to find them.

When I did, it was in the form of a gaggle of giggling grandmas that fawned over me while they wrestled with their giant sun hats and dog leashes. It wasn't so bad. Fans are fans. But after an unbearable half an hour with them, I was relieved to return to my emcee duties on stage.

The rest of the afternoon consisted of begging for donations and reading raffle ticket numbers. By six o'clock I was tired of standing on that rickety trailer and looked longingly towards my car. When the crowd finally thinned, the PPC began to break down their tents and booths.

***

As the carnival was wrapping up, Greg, Reilly, Sue, and I huddled into the back of the production van to throw together a rough cut of footage from the event.

It was much easier to do while still fresh in our minds. Sue scribbled an outline and various notes while Reilly took charge of the editing. I sat next to Sue, contributing next to nothing.

I'm usually not in the habit of smelling people, but Sue emitted this powerful scent of lilac and more than once I found myself leaning into her, drawn in by her aroma.

Greg sat in the corner with a small cooler of beer. With his camera work finished, he was taking advantage of the downtime. After a few minutes of hearing him slurp on a bottle neck, I caved and joined him.

"Reilly, you're too young to have one, but I suppose Hot Shot can partake?" I looked at Sue.

"Huh? Oh, no thanks. If you have some carrot sticks and a Fresca in there then pass them my way. Otherwise, have fun."

"You don't drink, Hot Shot?" I egged her on.

"Not cheap-ass light beer."

"Oh, more of a white wine type of girl?"

"When the moment presents itself? Yeah, I suppose I am." She looked a bit flustered. It was almost as if she had given me too much info. "I mean, I drink beer sometimes, not that skunk though."

"Fair enough. More for me," Greg said.

We spent another hour or so editing before the gang decided to call it a night. Sue and I hopped out of the back of the van to go find our cars. Within seconds of the rear doors shutting, Greg tore out of the parking lot to drop Reilly off at the station. I set my sights on my Land Rover in the distance.

"See ya Monday, Hot Shot," I called over my shoulder.

"Yep," Sue replied.

I should have offered to walk her to her car given it was getting dark. It didn't occur to me until I was twenty feet away from her and thought it would be too late to rebound with chivalry. Instead, I looked back several times to make sure she was safe as I got to my vehicle.

When I got there, I reached in my pocket to find a distinct lack of car keys. I checked every pocket, to no avail. Then I checked every door handle, frantically pulling up and down on each one.

Then I saw them—my keys, dangling gingerly from the ignition. I scanned the inside of the SUV and was even more disappointed to see my cell phone sitting plainly on the passenger seat.

I quickly turned to look for Sue, the last person left in the parking area with me. At first, I didn't see her. But soon I spotted the parking lights on her car fire up. She began to pull out of her parking spot to leave. I had to stop her.

Running from behind my SUV, I charged toward her car, waving my arms in the air like a lunatic. It was dark and she didn't notice me, so in a state, I pulled off one of my shoes and chucked it at her car window. She immediately slammed on her brakes.

I ran to the car. I must have caught Sue off-guard because as soon as I reached the driver's side window she left out a shrieking scream and covered her face.

Afraid of causing too much of a scene I gently tapped on the window and yelled "Hot Shot. Hot Shot! *Sue!* It's Jack. Calm down." For the first time since the car stopped she looked me straight in the eyes. Her entire body seemed to rise with the deep breath she was taking. She pressed one palm hard into her chest and sucked in more air before rolling down the window.

"Jesus, woman, it's only been, like, two seconds since we saw each other."

"What the hell are you doing?"

"I'm locked out of my car. Do you have a cell phone?"

"You threw your shoe at my car! It scared the crap out of me."

"Yeah sorry, I didn't want to get stuck here all night and I panicked. Cell phone?"

"Yeah...no, I don't have one." She pinched the bridge of her nose. "Get in. I don't live that far, you can use my house phone. Hurry up."

Without saying another word, I took a few steps back to coolly retrieve my shoe and circled around to the other side of Sue's car. She had to move her bag from the passenger seat before I could climb in and get comfortable.

"Seatbelt," she said without looking at me. At that moment my palms were starting to sweat. I struggled to buckle up, like a kid on a first date. It was a weird feeling, having a girl make me nervous. I thought I must be getting sick.

"So, you live around here?" I asked.

"The bungalows over off third."

"Yeah, those aren't bad."

"You've spent some time over there?"

"Sadly, I get around." I looked out the window to hide my smug grin.

"Oh I know, Rockefeller Rogers. You have a reputation, my friend."

Before I could say anything, Sue pulled out of the parking lot and proceeded to run through a stop sign.

"Woah! Okay, okay. I changed my mind. I think I'd rather walk." I started to jokingly pull up on the handle of the door when Sue sped up a bit.

"Stop being a baby."

"Okay, fine. But since we're moments away from a fiery car accident, my dying wish is for you to tell me where you heard about the name Rockefeller."

"You care that much don't you?"

"No...well kind of," I said.

"I went to Taft. It doesn't take long for word to spread about a guy like you."

Finally, it all made sense. Sue Anderson went to school a few towns away from me, a few towns from where we worked. I looked at her as she drove us to her place. I strained my brain to try and place her.

"I don't remember you," I said.

"Sounds about right. I don't know why you would. I wasn't in your target audience."

"Well that just makes me sound conceited."

"If the shoe fits."

***

We drove the rest of the way to her place in silence. I wondered quietly to myself if I had changed at all since high school. I thought I had matured, at least a little.

Sue was right, her neighborhood wasn't very far away and before I knew it I was hovering behind her as she struggled to unlock the deadbolt with her keys. She jiggled the key several times before it caught and she pushed the heavy wooden door open.

Inside was an eclectic mix of modern furniture and vintage art. It wasn't messy, but tactfully cluttered. It almost reminded me of my grandma's house.

The black leather couch was holding up an old faded green afghan and a small fireplace sat at the far end of the room, blackened from years of use.

"This place looks like Mama Cass and Elliot Smith had a baby and it gave all of its furniture to you."

"The phone is in the kitchen," she said as she twisted on a lamp near the door.

"Thanks." I crossed the room to the kitchen. It was one of the cleanest kitchens I had ever set foot in. The appliances were ancient, not uncommon for a rental, but well kept. The place felt like a museum diorama on life in the fifties. Sue made it feel warm and cozy by adding little pictures clipped from magazines and magnets to the otherwise mauve nothingness.

I picked up the phone and realized I had no idea who to call.

"Do you have a phone book or something around here?" I called to the other room.

"Um...I don't think so. I have a laptop in my room, though," Sue called back.

I rested the phone receiver back onto its base and returned to the living room. Sue was busying herself by lighting the bag of a small fake log inside of the fireplace. A series of twigs and logs were piled high around it. I stood patiently, watching her work the fire into a steady flame.

"That's pretty impressive. Most girls would have asked for help with something like that."

"Yeah, well, I'm not most girls."

"That's for sure, Hot Shot."

Sue stood up and stabbed her finger into my chest. "I told you to stop calling me that!"

"You left a TV station in a huge market to move back home to this shit hole town. I think it's a pretty good description. People only called me Rockefeller because my parents had money. I never earned that."

She bit her lower lip. Then she held out her hand as if to shake mine. I must have had a stupid look on my face, because eventually she grabbed my arm with her other hand and forced a handshake.

"I'm Sue Anderson. Nice to meet you." It took me a minute to recognize the truce she was offering, but I decided I had better take the offer while it was on the table.

"Jack Rogers. The pleasure is all mine." Standing there holding her hand, I subconsciously I fell into my playboy ways and flashed my pearly whites at her.

She cracked the slightest of smiles before she pulled her hand away and disappeared down the hall. When she returned, she was carrying her laptop and had a small knit throw draped over her shoulders.

It took us a few minutes to find a suitable locksmith on the web to call. By suitable, I mean, we chose based on the name Sue found least shady: Charles Falstaff. When I called, they told me I would have to wait at least two hours for them. I considered having Sue drop me back at my car to wait, but it was almost ten o'clock at that point and already getting pretty cold outside. In late October, the temperature dipped drastically after the sun went down.

Sue must have seen the decision brewing in my eyes.

"Jack, you can stay until they come, tell them to come here first. It's fine really." As she said this, I could look at nothing but her mouth. She really was quite beautiful.

"You've already been way nicer to me than I deserve. I wouldn't want to intrude."

"You already have," she said. "It's okay, really."

"Well in that case, you got anything to drink?"

Sue disappeared into the kitchen. The living room was starting to warm up from the fire and the light was casting odd shadows around me. Aside from the couch, there weren't any other chairs in the room, so I settled on the rug in front of the fireplace. It was soft, woven cotton in a starched blue. It felt good as I pressed my elbows into the weaves. Before long, Sue materialized with a bottle of wine and two glasses.

I liked where this was heading, but I forced the smile off my face and took the bottle from her hands. I pulled off the wrapper and she produced a corkscrew. Minutes later, she was sprawled on the floor under her throw and we both had full glasses of Pinot Noir.

"Should we have a slumber party?" I joked.

"I bet that line's worked before, hasn't it?"

"Well not those exact words, but pretty much."

"Man," she said, "it must suck to be so good-looking."

"We all have our struggles."

"But seriously. I bet you use your looks to take advantage of people, don't you?" she said.

The question kind of caught me off guard. I wasn't sure if she was trying to decide whether to sleep with me, or if she was being judgmental.

The expression on her face didn't reveal the answer, one way or the other. She propped herself up on a pillow and took a slow drink from her wine as she stared me down. It was a casual stare...almost as if she didn't care if I answered her or not. Perhaps she was daring me to battle back.

"You put that right out there, didn't you? I mean, it isn't like you're a troll or anything. I'm sure you get your fair share of attention."

"Maybe, but I don't date."

"Neither do I, but it doesn't stop me from having sexy time with loads of women. The consenting kind."

"Oh I don't doubt it." Sue shifted her weight and moved to refill her glass.

"So what is it? You're married to your job?" I said.

"Ha! Like I would open up to you." She scoffed.

"What? It's okay for you to ask me about my sex life, but I can't ask about yours? Kettle to pot, you're black too. Come on, I'm a good listener."

"I'm hungry. Are you hungry?"

"Uh, yeah I guess so."

"There's a big bowl of strawberries in the fridge. Be a lamb and go grab it."

She was being very direct and playful. I didn't argue. In fact, I kind of liked it. I jumped up and headed for the fridge. I pulled it open and was greeted with a health nut's delight. This thing was stocked from head to toe with yogurt, juice, fruits and veggies of all kinds. There was scarcely any processed food. I respected her discipline. I certainly was one to take care of my body too, so it was nice to see a complete commitment to the practice. I located the aforementioned strawberries and strode back to the living room.

"Quite the spread you got in there. I mean I can tell you're fit, but you could open up a farmer's market in your kitchen."

She stuck out her tongue before squeezing a strawberry between her teeth.

"So, Sue Anderson. This is what we're going to do. I'm going to tell you a story and then you can tell me one of your own."

"Do I need to hold a flashlight under my chin when I tell mine?"

"Come on, kid. It'll be way more interesting than listening to you talk about salad and work all night."

Sue sat up and crossed her legs. She glared at me for a minute. I think she was trying to read my motives. I sat stoic, trying to decide on my own intentions.

"Okay...fine. Tell me a story," she said.

My body relaxed when she gave me the thumbs up, I was finally starting to feel comfortable around this girl. I took a shot and pulled off my shoes. She didn't blink, so I joined her once again on the floor. I refilled my wine glass and pointed the bottle towards hers. She quickly pulled hers to her chest, careful not to overdo it.

"Let's see." I thought for a moment. "Once upon a time..." I quipped. Sue didn't immediately react, but her gaze was still firmly settled on me.

I continued, "Once upon a time there was a little boy named Jack. His Dad, Mitch, was 'The Hammer King' and ran the town's hardware store. Jack was the pride of the family. Except for Uncle Scott, who was threatened by him. Scott wanted to take over the hardware store for himself, but now Jack stood in his way."

Sue let out an exasperated sigh as she inspected one of her strawberries. I watched her as she gently plucked the stem off and tossed it back in the bowl.

"Why did you stop? Go ahead, keep going," she said.

"Right. One day Scott managed to convince Jack and his friend Nat to leave the store and explore an old bus graveyard nearby."

"A bus graveyard?" Sue wrinkled up her nose at the thought.

"Shh. Listen to the story, there will be time for questions later. Now, what they didn't know was Scott had tricked the kids into the bus graveyard. Luckily, Mitch rescued the kids before any harm befell them."

The next day, furious that Jack was still around, Uncle Scott lured him to a secluded lot under a nearby bridge. The plan was to stampede a herd of homeless people under the bridge."

"Are you kidding me..." she said.

"Shhh. Again Mitch managed to come to Jack's rescue, only he wasn't so lucky himself. After pushing Jack to safety, he was trampled to death. Scared, alone and taking blame for his father's death, Jack ran away to the city.

"Now while Jack was in the city, he was befriended by a skinny guy named Simon and a portly fellow named Paul. Simon was a bike messenger and one day on a delivery gone wrong, was accosted by his client.

Luckily, Paul and Jack happened by only to discover the client was Nat, Jack's childhood friend! After an enthusiastic reunion, which included some heavy petting and a little tongue, Nat told Jack what had become of the store while he was away. Things had gone to shit, the store was tanking fast.

"Nat urged Jack to return and reclaim his place in the town and save the store. So Jack gathers his crew and charges back to town to confront his Uncle.

"In a triumphant move, he hangs Scott over the side of a mighty pile of sheet rock and, in front of the entire staff, reveals the truth about his Dad. Scott pleads for his life and just as Jack is about to spare him, Scott takes one last punch at Jack. He moves at the last second and shoves his Uncle over the edge.

"The employees of the hardware store erupt into applause and Jack assumes ownership of the store. The End."

Sue sat in silence as I emphatically finished the conclusion of my tale. "That's it?" she asked.

"Un....huh." I slowly confirmed.

"That didn't happen."

"What do you mean? It was terrible, awful memories."

"So that was basically the movie, *The Lion King*, you changed the names and set it in small town America. Completely ridiculous, you owning a hardware store? Really? It's like you didn't even try to be sincere. Plus, it's a little creepy you know that movie so well."

"Okay, fine. My little sister watched it all the time when we were kids. But it's at least plausible. Can you do better?"

Sue filled her glass with the remains of the wine. She held the bottle over her glass for a few extra seconds to capture every last drop. When it stopped dripping, she licked the rim of the bottle before setting it down.

"You want to hear a story? Okay, I've got a doozy of a story," she said.

I repositioned my spot on the rug and extended my arm far enough to chuck a fresh log into the fire. As I settled back into my seat, Sue began to speak.

"When I was eighteen and a freshman in college, I started gaining weight, like a lot of weight. Well, a lot for me anyway. At first I thought it was your typical freshman fifteen, but at the same time something didn't feel right. I would get fatigued really easy and sometimes I would get awful heartburn. This kept up for a while, but I told myself, it was probably the cafeteria food or something, so I brushed it off.

"But then one day, I was walking back from class down this big set of concrete stairs, probably a good twenty or thirty steps and I got lightheaded. It was the kind of lightheaded that sends chills up your spine and makes everything get fuzzy around the edges. At first, it was sort of fascinating, like I was flying. I had no good reason to feel this way and it was the middle of the day, so I ruled out being roofied.

"Later, I realized I had fainted and my 'flying' was actually falling down the stairs. I was a little sad I couldn't really fly.

"I got pretty beat up rolling down the stairs, but luckily I didn't break anything. Even then, I wasn't quite ready to admit something was actually wrong with me."

Sue paused and took a sip of her wine.

"I'm failing to get the joke. I thought we were having fun here, are you being serious right now?"

"Do you want me to stop?"

"It's just...no, go ahead and finish." The air had been taken out of the room, but at the same time I wanted to know how the story ended. What had she been through? Was she better? Was she making the whole thing up?

The fact she was telling me this made me want to be anywhere else. It was unsettling.

She continued to go into detail about the months of doctor's appointments and her eventual diagnosis. Her voice was clear and articulate. I could tell she went through the details over and over in her head. She wasn't lying, there was too much truth in her tone.

"Sorry to interrupt," I said, "but I don't know what that is? It is serious?"

"Let's put it this way, about nineteen percent of patients die in the first year. Half die by the fifth year."

"Shit. And you've had it how long?"

"Seven years."

The words came out of her mouth like a jack-hammer, fast and irregular.

"You aren't lying? Please, tell me you're lying."

She laughed for a minute, refusing to make eye contact, "You don't know how many times I've wished that."

"Why are you telling me this? Does Earl know?"

"I didn't tell him. It's the reason why I came back home. I've been having more episodes recently, so I thought it might be a good idea to be close to my family. You know, in case I ran out of time..." Her voice trailed off.

We found ourselves sitting in silence, watching the new log burn and flicker in the darkened room. I definitely wasn't used to anyone dropping a bombshell like that into my lap. I wasn't sure what to do, so I cleared the wine out of my glass in one big gulp.

There was a part of me though who wanted to reach over and hold her tight, tell her everything was going to be fine. Looking at her, I knew better. It had hardened her somehow. She wasn't going to let me, of all people, see her cry. My guess was she had shed plenty of tears already, and had come to terms with it all.

As we sat in silence, each passively thumbing our wine glasses, the phone rang. It startled us both and I got up to answer it. I stood above her and Sue smiled at me as she mouthed the word *sorry*. I was sorry the evening suddenly turned awkward, but I wasn't sorry she told me the story.

From the kitchen, I projected my voice into the living room. "Sue, it's the locksmith, he's outside. You gonna be okay?"

She had already perked up and was stoking the fire with a metal poker as I came back into the room.

"I'm fine Jack, really. I'm sorry. I shouldn't have, I got a little carried away. I don't handle my wine I guess. I didn't mean to make this more awkward than it already was."

I moved towards her and she instinctively took a step backwards.

"Jack, you want to know why I don't have a boyfriend?"

"Not really, no."

"I'm afraid the second I fall in love, I'm going to die. I don't think I could stand it, leaving someone alone like that. It doesn't seem fair. I'll never allow anyone to get that close."

I stood there not sure what to say. I still am not sure why she confessed her greatest fear to me that night. Maybe she could sense that I was entertaining the idea of giving her a shot.

There I was, about to leave the Sue's house, and it suddenly seemed like the biggest mistake of my life. I didn't care about hooking up anymore. She was dangling before me like a marionette. She was vulnerable and while I sincerely doubted I would make a difference, I wanted to stay and find out.

"I could stay for a while if you wanted me to?" I said.

"No, you don't have to. I didn't tell you all that stuff so you could feel sorry for me. Honestly, I don't know why I told you...also, I'm not going to sleep with you."

"There's the Sue I know. Come on, it's not like that. I just thought...if you wanted to talk some more?"

"I'm good. I've got a nice warm fire to keep me company. Go on, it's fine."

"You know; women use the word fine when things aren't really fine. Last chance, I can stay if you want?"

Sue moved away from the fire and proceeded to push me towards the door. I fought her off playfully and then submitted to her shove.

"Okay, don't say I didn't ask. You have a lovely evening, Miss Anderson."

"Same to you Rocka....Jack Rogers."

And with that I left. Charles Falstaff himself drove me back. Eighty-five dollars later, I was in my car. I ended up driving to the bar to have another drink. Normally I would have sought the company of others, but I sat at the edge of the bar, drinking alone. My mind was free of all the usual work bullshit. All I could think about was how much longer she had to live.

I drove home, went to bed, and vowed not to give it another thought. It wasn't like I could have changed anything.

***

I couldn't shake her from my mind. Monday morning, I made it into the station far earlier than I was accustomed. I hoped I would find Sue there. I wandered the newsroom for a while and eventually found her in the copy room.

"Morning, Sue!"

"Oh! Jack, what in the world are you doing here so early?"

I lied and said, "I'm looking for my golf gloves, I was thinking of getting nine holes in before the news. How're you doing?"

She stopped me right there, "Let's not do this okay? I'm fine. It's not your problem."

"Sue, you can't tell me something like that and pretend like it never happened."

"I don't want to be your charity case. I'm fine. I am perfectly capable of doing my job..."

"Listen, so what? You have a bum heart. We all have our things. I don't intend to baby you if that is what you think. I still expect you to get your shit done and make me look good."

We stood there for a moment, my olive branch handed to her. I took a deep breath, and Sue cracked a smile. She then softly laid her hand on my chest, nodded and walked out of the room.

The rest of Sue's time at the station was fairly uneventful. For the next two years I kept her secret and she treated me with dignity and respect when no one else was looking.

I learned a lot about humility from Sue Anderson.

It was good for my overall character. She taught me never to make excuses for myself and to go the extra mile, even when I didn't want to.

Eventually she moved on. She was offered a job a few hours away to revive an aging network news affiliate. Last I heard, they had won several regional Emmy's and I suspected it was all Sue's doing.

I still think about her from time to time. If and when I decide to settle down, there's a fair chance that the girl foolish enough to stick with me will in one way or another be compared to Sue. It's a silly thought, and in some ways I hate her for it, but I can't deny its true. So what if she is a model for all that is decent?

I lost touch with her over time, as colleagues do. It wasn't like I went out of my way to stay close to her either. I did my thing and she dutifully did hers. I wouldn't describe what we had as a friendship, probably more of a mutual esteem.

I knew Sue Anderson. And for one night I knew her a little deeper than I should have, but only because she allowed it. I will always take that with me.

CHAPTER SEVEN
Josie 2007

I refer to myself as a 'Tattoo Artist' around certain friends and family. Tattooer, Tattooist, or Tattoo Girl makes it sound like I didn't made the right life choices, at least around the uninitiated.

Not that I'm prissy or anything. I listen to Black Flag for Christ's sake. When I hang out with the guys from my shop, I'm Tank Girl, Ink Bitch, I am the tattoo culture. But at the same time, I guess I don't wholly embody what you might think of when you think of tattooing.

Lewis, the owner of Greedy Ink, where I call home, is always giving me shit. It's hard enough being the only girl in the shop, but I also get a lot of flak for not being covered head to toe in tats. So I'm maybe a little bit selective, indecisive even.

The truth is I only have one tattoo.

I still deserve points because while it technically was done in one sitting, it is an entire sleeve covering my left arm, so I'm still a badass.

Working at a tattoo parlor does give me a certain amount of license to judge each and every one of you who comes in to get work done. And we call it 'work'. I'll snicker and scoff behind your back if you call it a 'tat' or 'ink' even though we call them that when you aren't around.

Tattooing is a very social job to have. I get up close and personal with people from all walks of life, and in various stages of having not showered. So you have to build up a bit of a wall around you to deal with whatever surprise may walk through the door.

I don't one-hundred-percent agree with the practice, but Danny and Mike, who work the stalls on either side of my me, have formed a sort of evil persona when dealing with the tattoo virgins of the world.

Sue Anderson fit this description to a tee. I was leaning against the 1950s dull red brick that made up the Greedy Ink's exterior smoking a cigarette when she walked past me and towards the shop door. She was strictly a 'walk-in' because she didn't have an appointment.

The tattoo industry was becoming a bit more respectable, or at least we wanted it to be. The expectation was that a patron called ahead and made a consultation.

That gave procrastinators like me time to size up the client, sketch out some ideas and schedule a time to have them come back and actually get the work done. This was priority number one, especially for large pieces that needed a lot of time to sort out.

That isn't to say we never get walk-ins and, if there's an opening, I'll honestly do my best to make the time. That's cash money, especially for a girl living a studio apartment in a questionable area of town. Besides, one more tattoo in the world is never a bad thing.

In most cases, the virgins are the walk-ins, they don't know any better. Which is why the guys like to give them the most shit.

It's cruel, sure, but it makes the day go by. It isn't as bad as it sounds. It isn't like we pour pig's blood over anyone's head. Truth be told, I try to stay out of it. It's mostly lame. Of course I can't say that out loud, boy's club mentality and all.

When I saw Sue, wearing designer sunglasses and a fresh white v-neck, she stood out. Her stride hesitated a moment at the double glass doors leading into the shop. We tattoo artists can smell fear. I couldn't help but follow her inside, as something told me there was going to be a shit show. I pinched my cigarette butt against my chucks and the sidewalk and slipped through the still open door behind her.

It didn't take long for Danny to perk up at the sound of the bell on the door, poking his head out of his stall. Sue stood oblivious at the counter, completely avoiding the walls of pre-printed tattoo designs. Maybe she had an appointment after all.

"Can I help you?" Danny called from across the room. He didn't see me at first, so edged myself against the wall to quietly observe.

"Uh, well I think so. Who do I talk to about getting a tattoo?"

"Do you have an appointment?" he said with a bit of a scowl. Danny was a teddy bear, but he tried really hard to look and act mean, it played well with his primarily biker-based clientele.

"An appointment? Oh, didn't think I needed one." She started to kind of contort her body in a manner that would suggest she was trying to be attractive. It wasn't a bad move, but Danny had already decided to sink his teeth into her regardless of how pretty she was.

"Well that's okay. Why don't you sit over there for a minute, and I'll have Mike come get you set up, okay?"

This was code for scare the shit out of the girl. The second Danny ducked his head back into his cubby, I launched myself into the corner of the room, hidden behind a stack of chairs. I glanced back at Sue as I made the move and she followed me with her eyes. I gave her a sly grin and pretended to reattach a poster on the wall.

I already knew what was going to happen. I could hear Mike telling his client in a hushed voice to hold tight for a minute, he had to go do something important. I shut my eyes and took a deep breath. It's all fun and games I told myself. At the same time, I realized my afternoon appointment was cancelled and I could use the cash from a walk in.

I was reconsidering my hiding spot, thinking maybe I should bail the poor girl out. Before I could step in though, Mike had already made his way to the lobby.

I decided to head for my stall and as I passed Mike, I gave him a disapproving frown. He put his finger over his mouth and gave me a calming shush. I could hear his footsteps stopping as I turned the corner.

"Hey. What's your name?"

"Sue." She responded with hesitation. Mike wasn't quite as much of a teddy bear Danny was. He was covered in tattoos of all genre and sizes, ranging from demons to naked ladies. He kept his jet black hair pulled tightly into a ponytail and kept a grisly looking beard to match. If you didn't really know him, he was definitely someone who looked scary. First impressions are a bitch.

"You sure you're in the right place?"

She laughed for a split second. "Well I hope so."

"Well, we don't do fucking butterflies and peace signs around here so maybe you're better off across town at Lucky Hand." It was abrupt and angry and punctuated with a hand motion that suggested she scoot along back to class. At first she gave a nervous laugh and then when Mike didn't budge she attempted to bite back.

"What about hearts?"

Danny and I poked our heads out to watch at exactly the same moment. Sue's face was hot and Mike's whole body shook with laughter. It was a simple test really. Bark back and get what you want, put your tail between your legs and get put out on the sidewalk. It was looking like this chick had a little fight in her yet.

"It's a God damn shame. Your skin's perfect for ink, you're pretty damn good looking too. But you have terrible fucking taste. Get along now, we can't help you." Mike turned and started to head back into his cubby.

"What would you know about it?" she retorted under her breath. She stood with one foot stepping on the other and was already looking towards the door. It was at that moment I hoped she could lick her wounds and figure out how to stick around.

Mike must have heard her grumbling, because he turned around and decided to have one more go at the poor girl.

"Listen," he said, "I create custom tattoo art. My stuff has been in magazines and I'm booked for appointments until the end of the year. I only work on pieces I can be proud of. This isn't spring break, we don't do rainbows and unicorns. We. Can't. Help. You."

She took one step closer to Mike and looked him right in the eyes.

"Prove it. If I'm that obnoxious, kick me out then. I came for a tattoo, and I intend to get one."

That was all she needed to say. Mike's scowl turned in a grin. He searched the room until he found me and Danny's floating heads sticking out of our stalls.

Looking at me, but talking to her, he said, "Alright then. Josie here will take care of you. I think she has a few hours free this afternoon."

I stepped back out into the lobby as he turned and disappeared into the back room. Sue and I were left standing there sizing each other up. I brushed my bleached blonde hair out of my face and moved to the counter.

Looking back, I think she was relieved to find another girl in the place, but I didn't give a shit. I was hard to be friends with in general, let alone with other girls. I glared at her, looking for a reason to confirm the hate I wanted to have for her. I had convinced myself that she came from money. What could we possibly have in common? She was a paycheck to me, nothing more.

Finally, after getting no read from her face whatsoever, I offered, "Come on."

I headed back towards my cubby. She followed me without saying a word. She must have thought she had already pushed her luck as far as it would go with Mike.

The room where I tattooed was small, but functional. There was no door, but the room opened to a few framed pieces of art and a bulletin board covered what little wall space I had. In the middle of the room was a glittered red tattoo chair that could unfold into a bed, given the angle I needed. I had a small desk where my laptop sat and a lamp. Running across the back wall was a narrow counter with a tiny sink sitting under a series of cabinets. Inside of the cabinets were my supplies: fresh needles, spare tattoo guns, ink, towels, Oreos that I kept hidden from the guys. The essentials.

I pretended to shuffle a stack of papers. Then I moved a few items from one side of the counter to the other, mimicking important things that needed to happen. I turned to find her awkwardly standing at the door to my stall.

"Well, sit down and tell me why you're here." The statement came out a little heavier than I planned. But, she seemed to relax a little bit and I feared I welcomed her entire damn life story. Before she had a chance to speak I started. "So what's your name and what were you thinking of getting done today? And where?"

She moved to the tattoo chair, sat down and swiveled towards me casually. "Sue. I was thinking of getting a tattoo of the Tin Man's heart from the Wizard of Oz on my thigh. I brought a photo, but I'm open to changes."

"Show me the pic, I haven't seen that movie in ages." I was at least partially impressed that she wasn't going for something cliché. Sue handed me a folded up piece of paper with a still image from the film. There was nothing to the heart, it was cartoonish and red with a clock stuck in the middle. I smiled, this tattoo would be a cake walk. Sue beamed as I looked over the reference photo.

"Looks simple enough, I'll do it for two-hundred and fifty. Give me ten minutes to draw it up and then we can see what you think."

I eyed Sue for a moment and she nodded in agreement. This was always the most awkward part for me. For bigger pieces I sent the customer away for a few hours or worked on the drawing at home. But with easier pieces like this, something I could sketch out in no time at all, I usually did it in front of them. This almost always meant small talk.

"So...stupid question. I know this is probably going to be annoying, but I have to ask. How much is it going to hurt?" Sue said.

I cringed. "You're right, that's the most annoying question of all time. It depends on you, I guess. It's different for everyone. I'd like to think the thigh is a pretty fleshy area, so that should help." I put my head down and started to sketch the heart, looking occasionally at the photo she had brought for reference.

I wanted to stay tough and distant, but I could tell already Sue was a decent person and not some dumbass airhead. After a few minutes of silence, which I actually appreciated, I extended an olive branch.

"So why'd you choose our shop over any others in town? And why didn't you make an appointment? You should always make an appointment."

Sue leaned back into the tattoo chair and started to nibble on her fingernails.

"Well, truth be told, I wasn't really planning on getting a tattoo today or ever, really. I mean, I've thought about it before, even keeping that picture of it in my car, but never got the courage to do anything about it. But you know...it's been an awful week and I drive by this place all the time, so I said, you know what? Screw it. I guess I was in the right mood. Sorry I didn't make an appointment. I guess I didn't think it through."

"It's cool. I guess there are worse reasons to get a tattoo. Why was your week so bad?"

"Oh, nothing of note, really. But when you live with disappointment long enough, I guess it catches up with you sometimes."

"Preach. You seem like you have it pretty well together though, that's seems like some heavy shit. What could possibly be disappointing? You break a nail or something?" I knew I was getting too deep into this conversation, but my coffee cup was empty and I needed something to give me energy.

"Looks can be deceiving," Sue said.

I looked up from my drawing. Clearly I must have offended her. "Oh come on, I didn't mean it like that. I just meant that...I don't know. You're pretty, you're clean, you're a virgin. You seem safe."

"What makes you think I'm a virgin?"

"Ha. I mean a tattoo virgin. Trust me, I don't give two shits about your sex life."

Sue smiled slightly and relaxed into her chair. I stiffened a little, determined to get back to business. My sketch was almost finished and I still needed to set up my needles and ink.

"So how did you get into tattooing? I guess I didn't expect a girl to be here. Not that it's a bad thing, I'm super glad you were here, otherwise I might have turned around and left."

"I don't know. I was always into drawing and stuff. So I guess when I ran out of paper, I switched to painting and then I ran out of canvas. Then I ran out of walls to graffiti and before too long I found myself hanging out at a tattoo shop all the time. One thing led to another and here I am."

My finished sketch was, in my eyes, an exact replica of the image Sue brought in. When I showed it to her she took a deep breath and closed her eyes.

"It's a tattoo, not a C-section," I said.

She then said simply, "Let's do it."

That was all I needed to hear. I love it when a client has no changes and I can get to work immediately. I may have looked like a slacker or deadbeat to the untrained eye, but I was meticulous and organized when I was setting up my workstation.

Everything had its place, from the different needles to the pedal that controlled my machine. My machine—who I affectionately called "Curly Sue"—felt alive in my hand as I fired it up. By the time I was ready to put the needle to Sue's leg, she was shaved, prepped and had the stencil of her tattoo applied. All my equipment was exactly where I wanted it. I converted the chair into a table to make her more comfortable. No detail was left untouched. I was a badass tattoo ninja.

"Alright, are you ready to start?" I offered.

Sue looked at me with deep blue eyes. I thought at the time they were welling up with tears. She wrung her hands into tiny little fists and sighed.

"Before we start, I have to tell you something. I wasn't going to say anything, but I think it's important that you're aware. This tattoo is something that has been on a list I started a long time ago. I guess you could call it a bucket list. Up until recently I didn't think it was anything real, anything that I thought I really needed to do before I left this world.

"But life isn't giving me a choice anymore. I know that now. And I'm not telling you this to scare you. I have issues with my heart and my life may not be here next week, next month or even tomorrow. So I wanted you to know what it means to me. I've decided maybe it's time I start crossing things off my list. Also don't make it ugly." Then she closed her eyes and braced herself for the pain.

"Wait a minute...you aren't going to drop dead in my chair, are you? What do you mean by issues with your heart?" I asked the question lightly, but I was becoming concerned. "I think there is something in our release form about heart conditions, maybe we should look at that again?"

"I'm fine. I'm telling you for the finality of your work more than anything. I'm not planning on dying today. Plus, I'm not on blood thinners right now, so that isn't a concern. I have what's called dilated cardiomyopathy and it can be controlled with diet and exercise...mostly."

"But you've been on blood thinners before? I don't know, man. I mean I'm glad you told me, but it seems like you're leaving something out. I don't know if I can do this tattoo. It's too much of a risk for both of us." I slumped down on my stool.

I honestly wasn't sure what to do. Sue seemed like she was smart and didn't even look sick, so I didn't think anything terrible was going to happen. But on the other hand, I wasn't a doctor and that type of stuff is always hanging out under the surface ready to screw up a good time.

"What if you had a heart attack right in the middle of this? Dude, I would lose my job, might put me off my game for a while. I don't want to risk it."

Defeated, Sue started to stand up. "Fine. Don't worry about it. I felt like I had to tell you, if you can't do it, then I guess that's that."

Suddenly I felt a pang of guilt. I didn't say anything at first, but I held up my hand to stop her. I needed a minute to think. Sue sat back down at the edge of the table. I looked down at my hands and they were shaking. This is just about the worst thing that can happen to a tattoo artist. Shaky hands usually mean shitty work. I stood up suddenly and Sue jumped.

"I need a second. Please stay. I'm going to get a coffee and go talk to my boss. Can you wait here?" I said.

"Do what you gotta do. I'm here."

I didn't hesitate. I tore off my gloves and left Sue sitting on my table. Being in there with her was suffocating me. I did a beeline outside, settling for a cigarette instead of calling Lewis.

Do the tattoo or don't do the tattoo? The question ran through my mind like a squirrel in a nut factory.

I considered both sides of the argument. First, I settled on the ethics. I would be putting Sue and myself at risk if something is truly wrong with her and it surfaced during my session. Then I considered this poor girl's last dying wish to get what really amounted to a fairly simple tattoo. I figured I could hustle and get it done in under two hours, no worse for the wear.

Just do it, I thought to myself. I could really use the money and she knows her body better than me. If something did go wrong, I could tell Lewis she didn't tell me shit and I had no clue what happened. It might have been naive, but it seemed like a good plan at the time.

I took one last drag off my cigarette and went back inside. I passed the coffee station and had to take three steps backwards to stop and hastily fill up a fresh cup before heading back into my cubby. When I arrived, Sue was right where I left her, eyes fixed on the ceiling.

"Okay, listen up," I called to her in hushed tones. "I'm going to go ahead and do this. But if anything happens you never told me anything about your..." I made a heart shape out of my hands at the off chance Mike or Danny were listening.

"Yep. We're good." Sue then lay back down and took a deep breath. She had a huge grin on her face and for a moment I felt like a hero. I took my place back in my stool, set my coffee down and put on a fresh pair of latex gloves. I looked at Sue one last time to remind myself that this was a good idea. Then I counted to five out loud, and on five I touched the tattoo machine to Sue's thigh and pressed my foot on the pedal below me. The motor roared to life and Sue jittered.

"Don't move," I said firmly. Sue quickly obliged and remained still for the next thirty minutes. I focused hard on my work and neither of us spoke during that time. Somehow it became a race, almost like a game. Finish the tattoo before she keeled over dead. Occasionally, I paused long enough to check her breathing.

After another fifteen minutes, the tattoo was beginning to come to life and I almost forgot what all the fuss was about. The outline of the heart was complete and I was beginning to work out the shape of the clock.

Sue wasn't bleeding abnormally and wasn't showing any signs that would have given me pause. I made a big deal out of nothing. I stopped for a second and cracked my neck, it was sweet relief after being hunched over Sue's thigh for forty-five minutes.

I imagined I was about halfway done. I still needed to place the numbers and hands on the clock, then shade the outside of the heart in red ink. Then I'd do my standard spot check and polish. Another fifteen minutes passed and I was finally relaxed enough to speak.

"How are you feeling? Managing the pain okay?" She didn't respond. I tried again. "Sue, how's it going?" Nothing. I took my foot off the pedal and looked up. Sue lay motionless. I could see her chest rising and falling, but her breathing seemed suddenly very shallow.

"Sue?" I raised my voice again. Nothing. My nerves kicked in. I laid the machine down on the tray next to me and nudged Sue's leg with my elbow. This can't be happening, I thought.

I grabbed her leg with both my hands and firmly shook her. Her body slid back and forth on the table like a spoon over spilt salt. She was out cold. What did I do? I was screwed. I thought I was doing something good for this girl and it was biting me in the ass.

"Jesus!"

"What?" Danny hollered back from the other side of the wall.

"Help! This bitch passed out!"

Danny and Mike both flew into my cubby instantly, Mike giggling with his camera in tow.

"Oh shit, she's down. Is she your first? I haven't had one of these in a long time," Mike said.

"You don't understand," I cried. "She...she, I think she had a heart attack!"

"What? You're high, she's still breathing, look. Splash some water on her and wake her up," Danny said.

Danny was right, she was still breathing. That had to be a good sign. I charged to the small sink at the counter and cupped my hand under the tap. After filling it overboard a few times, I finally walked it slowly over to Sue and dumped it on her face. Immediately she gasped for air and her eyes flew open.

Mike started snapping photos and Danny cheered. I grabbed Sue's arm to keep her from falling off the table.

Danny spoke first, "Alright, alright. Show's over. I got work to do." After a few more photos both of them left the room.

When they left, I immediately stuck my nose into Sue's face. "What the fuck? Are you okay?" I lowered my voice into a hurried whisper. Sue started to come to, propping herself up onto her elbows.

"I don't know. I must have passed out. Sometimes that happens if I cut off circulation somewhere. I'll be okay."

"Well I'm super glad you'll be fine, but what about me?! I thought you died."

"I'm sorry," she pleaded. "At least I was sitting still so you could work? Are you finished?"

I couldn't figure out what to do with my hands at that moment. I was stressed and unnerved. It's funny. I've seen a person pass out before, but it had never happened on my table. And it sure didn't come with the inside information the person had a bad heart.

I settled on grabbing my coffee and taking a large gulp of caffeine. I sat there for a moment and then found myself staring at the wall in a trance. I could hear Sue calling my name, but I couldn't find a way to answer. Jesus, this girl really messed me up. Finally, she touched my shoulder and I snapped out of it.

"Sue...I can't finish this right now. I'm too wound up."

"Oh...okay. How much do you think I have left?"

"See for yourself," I said, pointing at her thigh. I grabbed a spray bottle of antiseptic and rinsed off her tattoo while I quickly wiped it down with a paper towel. It was a perfect grayscale heart with the guts missing, only a half-finished clock.

I managed to fill in the numbers from one to eight and the small circle in the middle from where the minute and hour hands would be born. It looked a little sad, but I didn't care. I wasn't going to fire up my machine again. I needed to lie down.

My eyes darted to Sue. She looked at the unfinished piece for a while. I couldn't tell if she was upset or angry.

"I'll wrap it up and maybe you can come back another time to finish it. It shouldn't take more than 30 minutes or so," I offered.

Sue looked up at me and I finally got a clear view of her face. It was red and her eyes were full of tears. I immediately reconsidered my decision. Why was this girl getting over on me?

"Okay, I guess we can finish now."

"No. I think I put you through enough today. Don't worry about it. I love what you've done so far, it means so much that you started it."

"Ugh! Why are you so nice? I hate not finishing. Let's just finish it now."

"Nah, I think we're done." She said as she slid to the edge of the table and dropped the extra six inches to the dingy tile below. "I'll call you sometime next week and we can figure out when I can come back to finish."

Then Sue reached into her pocket and pulled out $250, laid it on the table and walked out of the room.

"Do you want a receipt?" I called after her. She replied by ringing the bell to the front door of the shop on her way out. I scooped up the cash and started to slowly clean up my station, defeated. At one point, I realized I had tears in my eyes, for no reason whatsoever I was physically and mentally upset. I was drained.

This girl, a sick girl showed up to my tattoo shop with no appointment, with a grand agenda and passed the fuck out. And we both lived to tell the tale.

Weeks passed and Sue never called. Life gets busy I told myself. After a few months, I still couldn't stop thinking about her. I had convinced myself she was dead. Her heart finally gave out and she was lost to this world. After a year, Sue simply became a crazy story to tell folks when the subject of passing out during a tattoo came up.

But even after all that time had passed, every once in a while I still held out hope she would walk back into the shop, healthy and ready to finish her tattoo. I even turned down an offer to move to another shop because I was afraid Sue would come looking for me. I made that decision for a girl I knew for all of three hours. I was probably mental.

Then it happened. One morning I unlocked the front door of the shop. Being the first one in the shop meant that you had to collect the mail that came uncharacteristically early on that side of town. I bent over to gather the loose letters and set my coffee cup on the floor to make the job easier.

Right in the middle of the pile was a dark purple envelope addressed to me. It looked like a greeting card envelope and there were annoying little accent flowers drawn all over the corners. It also had no return address. I was fixated on the envelope as I crossed the room. I discarded the remaining mail on the front desk and walked into my cubby. I dropped off my bag and flipped on the lamp. Then I huddled over my desk, guarding the envelope like buried treasure only I knew about.

I turned it over in my hands a few times before tearing into it like a child whose mother told them explicitly not to open it. Inside was a single photograph. It was a sleeping Sue sprawled across a bed. She was naked, though sheets cleverly hid all the interesting bits. The sun came through a window at the right angle and it made her hair glow.

I knew it was her immediately, but it was all but confirmed when I saw the half-finished tattoo resting on her thigh. It was stark in the light of the room she was in, simple and bold on her fair skin. I ran my finger across the photo, feeling extreme regret for not sucking it up and finishing the damn thing.

Eventually, after staring at her for so long you could make the case for lesbian tendencies, I turned the photo over. On the back was a short note. It said:

Dear Josie,

I'm still here, only now I am more complete than ever.

Thinking of you,
Sue Anderson

I laughed through mounting tears and then pinned the photo up on my bulletin board. I never saw her again, and I decided I was okay with that. I had made an impact on her little part of the world and she on mine.

From that day forward, anytime a customer requested a heart, in any style, shape or color I jumped at the chance. They became my signature. Every single one reminded me of that afternoon with Sue. Every time I finished one, my own heart beat a little faster, anxious for what the future would hold.

IAN CAHILL

CHAPTER EIGHT
Daniel 2008

When she crawled out of bed the sun hit her blonde hair, causing the whole room to feel a little bit brighter. She was wearing the extra small Rainbow Brite t-shirt she had found in her old bedroom on a recent stop home.

I squinted a bit trying to fully wake, which forced a soft white glow around her. Her underwear was Easter-egg pink. The skin covering her legs below her butt was so smooth I had to fight myself not to reach out for it and tug her back to bed.

She told me she was late for work as she pulled on her pants. Part of me wished it were still raining so I would have the edge I needed to convince her back into my arms one last time.

When we fell under the covers the night before, it was a hectic and messy. Perhaps the six Jack and Cokes influenced my judgment. I tried to piece together what it took to put us both in that room. I rolled back over and pressed my head into a pillow. My eyes were beginning to adjust to the light.

It was all coming back. Barry invited her to his birthday party. She had deep blue eyes.

***

It wasn't my job to serve food exactly, but I was trying to class up one of Barry's lame parties. I couldn't help but stare at her as I served cheese and crackers to folks nearby. Her tight jeans and sweater fit her perfectly right. She had stuffed her feet into shiny black heels, which contrasted her hair, tousled into a bun at the top of her head.

When I found myself in a corner, I would turn my neck completely around in an effort to catch a glimpse of this girl. Once I turned my head so far that when I righted myself forward, I saw fireworks from the loss of blood.

Cheese tray in hand, I finally got the nerve to walk up to her. Barry's dog, Lon Chaney, had caught the scent of cheese and followed closely behind. He was a Labrador and his huge tail whipped furiously back and forth as he hurried to keep up.

She knelt down, adjusting the little black straps that held her shoe to her feet. I stopped above her. She didn't look up and I stood awkwardly waiting for her to return to my level. Lon Chaney pushed himself between my legs and she looked up. First at the dog, then at my quivering knees, then at my face. When our eyes met, I smiled.

"Cheese?" I said. She shook her head and declined.

"I'm Daniel. Collins."

"Sue Anderson," she motioned to Lon Chaney still lingering under me.

"That's Lon Chaney."

"Oh I know, we've met, he got a little fresh with me earlier," She giggled as I floated a few slices of cheese into the dog's face. He took them and proceeded off to the kitchen.

As her giggling faded, we held our stare. I casually put the tray of cheese down on a nearby table. And there we were.

She flipped her hair and looked past me for a moment. She could have been looking for her date; she could have spotted the birthday boy, Barry. As she looked through my pale skin and three-day-old shave, I reached out and pushed a piece of hair back behind her ear. She turned her eyes to me as I did this.

Sue stood there for a moment with her mouth open. I was mortified, but stood firm waiting for her next move.

"I'm gonna go find the restroom," she said.

I shouldn't have done that. It couldn't have been creepier. Defeated, I turned to find my cheese tray. Lon Chaney had found it first. I picked up what was remaining from the floor and headed to find another drink.

For the rest of the night, I scarcely saw Sue. I didn't know if she was trying to avoid me or not, but she was doing a wonderful job at it. She managed to squeeze into nearly every conversation in the room, be it political battle or Bundt cake recipe.

Approaching her became a game, and I was losing. Once I came within two feet of her with a glass of wine stretched out in her direction. At the last second she blurted out the chemical compound for cyanide, NaCN. She had apparently settled an argument between two guys wearing fedoras and Ed Hardy t-shirts.

After some time, I admitted defeat. I found myself on the large brown leather sofa in the corner of the room wondering if I was ever going to amount to anything in life. Picking up a girl at a party was one thing, but I was twenty-seven and still living like I was eighteen. I'd say I was in between jobs. In reality, I couldn't get a job because deep down I thought everything I applied for was beneath me.

My parents helped pay the rent, and I was still living on the last of a small inheritance from my grandmother. It was nearly gone and I had no next step. I was college educated and woke up at noon every day. It weighed on me, but I still wasn't ready to admit I was dangerously close to scraping the bottom of the barrel.

I not only finished off Sue's would-be glass of wine, but also a fresh Jack and Coke I had poured for myself. The room was beginning to fade when Sue sidled up next to me. I looked her up and down for a moment.

"You look happy."

"I am," she offered.

"Proud of your creepy knowledge of scientific formulas?"

"Oh you heard that? Not as impressive as it looks. My Dad used to make me recite chemical compounds all throughout high school. I think he thought it would repel all the boys if I were into science. My name's Sue by the way. Hi." She extended her hand towards mine as if we had never met.

I grinned, trying not to look anxious, though it must have been obvious. I offered her the empty wine glass. She tipped the stem of the glass towards the black and white streamers hanging from the ceiling, the byproduct of Barry's decorating attempts.

My eyes focused on her lips as the last drop of wine crawled down the glass and touched her tongue. Her head lingered upwards as the streamers swirled in the smoke and chatter around us. Satisfied, she looked into my eyes.

"You're cute," she said.

"I agree."

She laughed and the sound seemed to implode. The corner we were sitting in felt like it was suddenly closing in until she was halfway on my lap whispering her words into my cheekbone.

"I think you're cute, and I'm pretty sure you think I am too," she said.

She was drunk. Morally speaking, I was in no condition to feel bad for her, I was right there with her. As her wine-laced breath poured over my face and down my shirt, I moved closer.

Nothing mattered. Not my tragic unemployment, not my bank account or my sad, wrinkled button-down shirt. When I kissed her behind the ear, my world stopped. She didn't shy away, but didn't move closer either.

She put her hands on her temple and sat motionless for a minute.

I didn't dare move, eager to hear and feel her next move. When she looked up, she turned forward as if noticing, for the first time, a party taking place before her. Then, drunkenly, she pointed at a rather small, stocky woman in a teal skirt.

"Her name is Alice," she told me. "Alice just bought a new car, only on her way home from the dealership she hit a squirrel. She was devastated and couldn't bring herself to turn around and verify the death." Sue yawned as she told me this. "Alice drove the car for two days, before the guilt became too much and she took it back to the dealer."

Sue's eyes fluttered and she inched closer to me. My skin tingled as she wrapped her arms around mine. She put a finger to the tip of her nose as if thinking for a moment before she pointed at Barry.

"That's Barry. This is his party," she said.

"I agree."

"I met him at the bar at a restaurant last week and he invited me along. I wasn't even drinking, but it still came as a surprise when he asked me for a hand job later in the parking lot. When I said no, he calmly segued from hand job to house party. I thought twice about it, but came anyways."

Sue didn't look at me after revealing these tawdry details about my friend, none of which surprised me. I sat with her glued to my body in silence.

How did I possibly get in this position? With Sue, drunk and floundering, a casualty of Barry's sick mind. This must be what Sir Lancelot felt like. To want something so bad and having it right in your arms, but not being able to have it because it was already promised to someone else. I could feel a headache coming on, so I pressed my index finger hard into my eye.

My misguided kiss was a fond memory. Now, I felt as though I was stuck babysitting one very drunk and very chatty girl. The party was beginning to wind down and the big leather couch we had spent the better part of an hour on was still somehow pulling us closer.

As we sat, overlapping, I started wondering if Sue had passed out. Her lack of movement was causing my arm to fall asleep. Of course she was gorgeous and inviting, but I wasn't sure how much more of this I was willing to deal with.

I spotted a bottle of beer that appeared to be half full. I reached out for it, trying not to disturb her. It was no use, I grazed the brown glass with my fingertips, but that was as far as I got. A choice had to be made. It was either Sue or my sanity. I started to stand up.

The slightest movement of my hips against hers caused her to stir. Her eyes got big and she looked at me half embarrassed. She wiped a bit of drool on the back of her hand and attempted to stand up too. She promptly fell back into my lap.

She looked at me with the sweetest face, and I was reenergized.

"I have a bit of a headache," she said and laid her head on my chest, breathing out hard. "In fact, I've had a headache for the better part of eight years, five months." It was an odd thing to say, but regardless I moved my arm around her and squeezed tight. I wasn't ready to let her go.

The situation felt oddly normal, if I tried hard enough, I could have pictured us sitting on my own couch, watching TV before we called it a night and headed off to sleep.

It was at this point she kissed me. I was not ready for it and her intoxication lead her to kiss mostly the bottom of my nose. She moved over my body like a sheet blowing in the wind. I was immobile, I let her continue to kiss and tug at me. I kind of thought if I tried to move or kiss her back, that I would wake up and the whole thing would end.

I wanted to bang my head against the wall. Here I was, finally, doing what I had fantasized about all night, and I wasn't able to enjoy it. Sue's lips shifted back and forth over mine in hypnotic pensiveness. This kind of thing never happened to me and I was killing the moment.

Sue was driven by forces seemingly beyond her control. She was driven by alcohol, by sexual desire, by everything her mother told her not to be driven by. She didn't seem to notice my conflicting emotions as she guided my hand under her shirt.

She clearly wanted something exciting to come out of the night. Of course she was beautiful, that wasn't it. I guess my reason for hesitating was the possibility of love.

At this point, all she knew about me was my name and my calculated stares at her from across the room, and I wasn't convinced she remembered either. What she didn't know was that I wanted desperately to hold out for true romance.

I liked Sue, what little I knew of her. Though, I was unclear as to whether or not she even considered me boyfriend material. You would think this would matter very little, considering she was a buffet on my lap, but it was.

It was plainly obvious the intimate conversations we shared over the past few hours meant nothing, she was merely interested in sucking my face. Any normal guy would have been ok with that, and maybe I was too because I made little-to-no effort to stop her.

Sue found my erection through my pants with her hands and I could hear her breathing pick up as she rubbed up and down against it. Now my whole body was in cahoots with her. I had ideas, but wasn't sure how this was going to play out.

I considered several options after my penis betrayed me. I thought I would feign choking and get out of there before I did something to screw it up. Plan

B amounted to holding my breath until I passed out. What was I thinking? The pleasure was becoming unbearable. I told myself to let it happen, but something stupid and morally sound deep inside myself couldn't let her continue.

I needed to get up. With both my hands firmly gripped to her waist, I pushed her a good six inches from the tonsil rodeo she was competing in. I looked at her deeply and made the choice to stand up. I spoke no words and neither did she. Sue's eyes followed mine as I took a step.

I took two more and suddenly five. Before I could move any further away I stopped. With my lips still wet from kissing, it all became clear. We were two people making out at a party. A calm washed over me and I turned around.

***

Grabbing Sue's hand and pulling her into the guest bedroom was by far the boldest thing I had ever done in ages. Watching her in that little t-shirt and faded pink panties the next morning only confirmed it. It was more than likely she didn't have any feelings for me; maybe I had spent the night with Jose Cuervo or Jack Daniel, but would it matter in the long run?

I caught a glimpse of a heart tattoo on her inner thigh as she pulled on her vintage jeans, something I must have missed in the fury of the night. She kept her back to me as she finished dressing. I half expected her to sprint out the door without so much as a nod. I braced myself and pulled a pillow over my face. As I lay there, the pillow slowly suffocating me, I felt movement on the bed. I kept my eyes closed and held my breath.

Sue's body slinked over mine one last time and she pulled the pillow from my eyes. She hovered a moment, ensuring my attention and quietly kissed my lips and proceeded to whisper a heartfelt "thank you" into my ear.

I threw her a glowing smile as I lay there holding the weight of her entirely on my chest. She started to slide off of me, so I grabbed her hips and pushed her back on top. I held her in place for a moment.

"You can't leave."

Nervously she stared into my eyes. Her loud sigh announced that I had busted the perfect romantic get-away she had mapped out in her head. I sat up sliding her to my side.

"Who are you, anyways?" I said.

She ran her fingers through her hair, which now fell in massive waves around her face. I could sense I was making her uncomfortable.

"This was fun, right?" she asked.

"Uh...yes, this was amazing."

She fought off a smile and sat up straight on the bed. "Then that is who I am, just an amazing time and nothing more." She became vacant as she recited the words.

"Oh come on. You aren't getting off that easy. Last night was so...maybe a little messy, awkward and totally out of character for me."

At this she laughed, and I could see her cheeks growing red. She pulled a lock of her hair tight and positioned it at her lips. She had been had.

"I don't normally drink and last night was not status quo for me. I didn't mean to sleep with you...in fact..." her voice trailed off.

"In fact what?"

"Nothing. I gotta go, I'm late for work."

"It's Saturday. Where do you work?"

"We don't have to do this you know," she said.

"Do what?"

"Pretend like we care. We had sex, it was something. Can we leave it at that?"

I thought about it. I wasn't sure I wanted to. "Well I suppose that's one way to look at it...but why is it something tells me that would be out of character for you?"

"What makes you say that?"

"I don't know, I guess...you did turn down Barry and no one ever turns down Barry. As long as I have known him, he has always gotten the girl. But you said no to him. Seems stupid, but the fact that you didn't give him a hand job gives me true hope in this world."

"Okay, that's a fair point, but I was drunk last night and I wasn't when I met Barry."

"Right. Well, do you want to do it one more time before you go?" I looked the other way.

"What!"

"Well you said I was cute when you were drunk. I wanted to see where I stood when you were sober." At this she rolled her eyes, but then quickly righted them and gave me a tender look.

"I suppose you're cute sober too."

I reached out and put my hand on her knee, she quickly recoiled and inched closer to the edge of the bed.

Sighing, I responded, "Well for what it's worth, I don't do one-night stands. All I know is that I didn't want to leave your side last night and so what if it led to something maybe we both didn't plan? What I do know is I'd love to see you again. I thought if you wanted to have dinner tonight or something, maybe we could get to know each other a bit?"

At this Sue stood up and took one step towards the door. Then she walked back to the bed and sat down facing me.

"Do you have a girlfriend?" she asked.

"Um, no? Why would I?"

"Okay listen. You seem like a decent guy and I really do appreciate you wanting to take me out and I'm really sorry for acting so slutty last night. I was, uh, having a life moment. We both made choices last night, and I would be lying if I said I didn't let it happen. But I can't have dinner with you."

I laughed. "We both let it happen. I mean, I definitely hesitated as to whether or not I was taking advantage of you, but believe me. I wanted this too.

Please let me take you out, let me prove to you that one time wasn't the plan."

"Hey, I know it wasn't the plan, I came on to you! Let's agree we both had fun and move on. I would prefer it that way."

"It's just dinner. What is the big deal?" I was growing a little annoyed. I was not about to let her make me feel like a jerk for sleeping with her. She was right. She came onto to me.

"I don't want to make this weird. You don't need to feel obligated. I don't need anyone on my arm, it will just end in heartache."

"What in the world are you talking about?"

"I was a virgin, okay?!" She screamed this louder than I expected. I turned my head and squinted my eyes. When she was finished she got up and stormed out of the room. I struggled with the sheets for a minute and stumbled out after her. When I got to the door I called, "Sue, wait!"

She was halfway across the living room of the apartment when she turned around. Her eyes got wide as they passed over me.

"Um, you're naked." She held out her hands in an attempt to block my crotch from view.

I looked down and she was right. I was very naked. I turned and headed back into the bedroom to find my pants, all the while shouting, "Don't leave yet. I want to talk to you!" I found my pants and a t-shirt wadded up near the window. I quickly pulled on the pants, absent of my boxer shorts, and stormed through

Barry's third floor apartment fitting the shirt over my head. As I went I kicked a beer bottle and got tangled up in the remaining streamers from last night's party.

Sue was halfway down the stairs when I caught up to her. "Would you wait up?"

She finally stopped and immediately collapsed against the wall of the stairwell. She looked ashamed and worn out.

"Fine. I shouldn't be taking the stairs anyways," she mustered.

"If I would have known that I wouldn't have slept with you last night."

"Oh gee, thanks."

"Hey, I said last night. I would have...I mean I wouldn't have...been so careless. I would have tried to earn it."

She began to cry. Small whimpering tears that made very little noise. Her cry face was a contorted mess. The look on her face caused me to pause and reassess.

Did I really want to be sitting here on the stairs with her? Last night she was oozing sex appeal like an old pro, now she was blubbering like a fifteen-year-old girl.

Eventually, my instincts took over and I put my arm around her, pulling her closer to my chest. The circumstances that brought us together didn't really matter now. Here we were in a moment and it could mean anything. We could tell our kids about this someday, or

I could never see her again. It was overwhelming and, at the same time, cozy.

I could feel my shirt getting wet with her face pressing harder to my chest as she wept.

"There, there...I don't know why I said that. Can you calm down? Please. Someone might pop their head out and think I hit you or something."

She stopped for a moment and sat up straight, wiped her wet face with the palms of her hands and gave me a puzzled look.

"Don't you think I would probably have a different type of cry if you had hit me as opposed to you taking my virginity?"

It was a simple statement, but something about it gave me the chills. My breath was pulled out of my throat and my eyes grew with fear.

"What?"

"No, seriously does it sound like I am crying because of you or because of me?"

Sue was calming herself down with these questions. I considered the thought she posed, which calmed me down too, then offered up my own interpretation.

"Well now that I think of it, I suppose it doesn't really sound like you are so much upset with me. Maybe that would sound more screechy and high-pitched?"

"Right, I think my crying was more guttural, inverted even. Hmm."

We sat there, my arm still half hanging off her shoulder, both of us breathing heavy as the morning sun pushed its way into the corridor through a window high above us. I was at a loss for words. I wasn't sure if she wanted an apology or for me to go back upstairs and let her go home. Then she spoke.

"I didn't picture my first time like this," she said.

"I don't think it was all bad. I mean, I didn't even realize it was your first time until you said something today. You seemed to know what you were doing."

"Jesus, I don't care how I performed, dummy. I told myself years ago I never wanted to deal with this. I didn't want to share myself with someone else like this. I knew it would be amazing and beautiful and wonderful if I let it be and I think it was in a way. But then suddenly it wasn't."

"I don't follow. You keep saying 'like this.' What does that mean?" I said.

"I woke up this morning and felt something. I realized I wanted to be there in that bed with you. I wanted you and then I hated myself for it. I was disgusted I let it go that far. It was selfish and reckless."

"Hey, I don't mean to sound dumb, but I certainly wasn't disgusted. I don't think I understand where you are going with this."

"It's simple really. I'm past my expiration and it isn't fair to drag someone else into my world only to be crushed without notice. Don't get me wrong, last night was a memory that no one will ever be able to take from me. You were gentle and kind and exactly who and what I needed at that moment. But Daniel, you can't fall for me. I know that isn't fair and I know you can't choose who you love, but it can't be me."

Her words hung in the air. Love? I don't think I mentioned anything that important. Last night had begun as lust, a whole mountain of it. Sure, I wanted to avoid her advances in case there was something bigger hiding under the surface. Maybe she was thinking the same thing, before things escalated. But listening to her was basically confirming my greatest fear. She thought last night was a mistake.

"Sue, I just want to take you to dinner. No more, no less. We can let fate decide where the rest of the pieces fall. Last night was fun, but if that is as far as you want to take it, okay. But you don't have to paint me as a martyr or feel sorry for me. I'm a big boy."

Frustrated, she lightly punched me in the arm and sighed, "You don't get it. I don't feel sorry for you. It's me that's sorry. I thought I could forget about everything and cure it with sex. At some point last night, I was convinced that I was going to sleep with half of the city before it was all said and done."

"Oh," Was all I could muster and suddenly I felt ashamed of myself. I grabbed her hand in mine and squeezed, trying to hold onto some common thread. We sat there for a minute until our breathing was in sync, it was romantic and confusing. I wanted her more in that moment than I ever had and yet I knew it would never happen. She would walk out of the building and never come back.

"I'm only telling you because I did feel something for you. I'm glad it was you and not a million other guys, but I can't let you in. If we fell in love, and I'm not saying we will, but if we did, imagine how terrible it would be if I died tomorrow, or next month or on our wedding night? Your heart would be in no better shape than mine, torn into tiny pieces and I can't do that to you or anyone. I won't do it."

She said, "I'm sorry" and kissed me on the neck and then pressed her chin to her chest and trembled.

"Sue. We can't live our lives like that. We can't live like there's no tomorrow. We had fun last night. I needed it. I hadn't been with a girl like you in a very long time. It was nice to feel you and be with you. It doesn't have to lead to marriage. It doesn't have to mean anything you don't want it to. But I'd hate myself if you left here without at least a chance to find out what it means. Maybe not today, maybe not tomorrow, but someday you might want to see me again or fuck me again or whatever it is that we shared last night. Please let me give you my number and I'll let you make that choice."

The tears began to grow inside of her eyes again and she stood up. She stumbled for a minute and caught herself on my shoulder. I considered standing, but instead remained sitting on the edge of the stairs.

Her sobs became more pronounced. "I gotta go. I'm late for work, and I just...gotta go." She bent over and wrapped her arms tightly around mine. "I know this must have been award-winningly awkward and for that I apologize. I'm drained and maybe I'll see you around. Tell Barry thank you for inviting me."

She pulled away and rattled the bannister as she scampered the rest of the way down the stairs and outside. I sat and watched the door hang and slowly pulled itself closed, taking the daylight with it. I took a panicked breath and wiped away a slight outcropping of moisture that had gathered in the corner of my eyes. She was gone.

After some time, I found myself back in Barry's living room. It was littered with trash and somewhere in the apartment a soft pop song played. I was getting a headache and wandered into the kitchen to look for some aspirin. Standing inside the kitchen slurping on a bowl of cereal, was Barry. He was wearing a baby blue terry cloth robe and a shriner's hat. He nodded at me and took another bite.

"Good party then?" I said.

Through soggy flakes he said, "Absolutely. You didn't sleep with that Sue girl, did you?" His question caught me off guard.

"Yeah, I guess I did. She told me about your failed attempt at a hand job." I glared at him.

He grinned from ear to ear and his mouth pulled into a tiny circle as he said, "Oops. It never hurts to ask. But good for you, she was pretty sexy."

"Yeah and she was a virgin."

"Oh shit! No way."

"Yeah, and you wouldn't know it last night. She was like a pro in there."

"So it was good then?"

"Yeah better than good. But she told me this morning that she wasn't interested in anything, so now I don't know what to do."

"Ah, tough break kid. At least you got to taste the forbidden fruit at least once, you got one on me there. I slept alone in the fetal position last night." At this he tipped his hat over his eyes and took another large mouthful of cereal.

"I suppose so," I said as I sighed. "Listen, I'm gonna get out of here. Thanks for letting me crash. I'd wash those sheets if I were you."

"Duly noted sir, see ya later."

I fetched my shoes and wandered to my car thinking of nothing but the pale soft skin of Sue Anderson. Her face was burned into my brain for the next few months. I looked for her everywhere. For nothing but to say I was sorry for unfairly taking her virginity one more time.

Sometimes, when I have some time to reflect, I realize how heavy it must have been for her. She must have really been in a state to so casually give away something so important to someone like me. I'll never know what made her choose me that night, and probably never will.

Once, I was good enough for a smart, charming girl to give her purity to me. It makes me laugh whenever I think about it. I didn't deserve it.

I really would have taken her out. There was something about her I was drawn to. I try to tell myself she was merely some crazy chick I hooked up with. Maybe she had the whole virginity story worked up to fulfill some nutty sex fantasy. Maybe I was nothing more than a role in some psycho game. Maybe I'll never know the truth.

CHAPTER NINE
Jackie 2009

I never meant to stumble. I guess no one really does. It's the hard times, like Sue's disease, that bring a family together. Maybe it did at first, but then things went in a direction not even I planned for.

The night Dr. Norris called, asking to speak with Sue, lasted an eternity for me. It was the first time we finally had answers after months of anguish.

Sue had cardiomyopathy, and she was so young. At first, I couldn't exactly wrap my head around it. As a parent there are plenty of things that you don't feel equipped to handle, but this was the mother of all scenarios. My baby was dying.

I remember the family sitting somber at the dinner table trying to put it into perspective. My head was pounding from an all-day energy conference I had attended and I don't think I was mentally prepared to find out what we were dealing with. What she had to live with.

I knew the fatigue and fainting Sue was experiencing wasn't normal, but I didn't dream it was the result of a serious heart condition. That was part of the reason we let Sam take Sue to her appointments, Don and I hoped it was simply stress and anxiety might have been the culprit.

Don and I handled it in very different ways. That night my answer was a 1974 Montbray Riesling. I drank it slow and deliberately until I couldn't keep my eyes open.

In the weeks that followed, we had made the decision to continue to keep Sue at the house while she saw the doctors and worked on creating a routine that would not only keep her alive, but ideally strengthen her heart over time.

Now that I knew what we were up against, my analytical side kicked in. I craved information, reading as many studies and reports as I could on dilated cardiomyopathy. I also became more involved in Sue's doctor appointments, eventually taking time off work to escort her to each and every one.

At the time, I was a consultant for a small company named Yingli Solar. They were working on advancing solar module production for the commercial market. I immediately cut my travel time in half and starting camping out at the doctor's office. Eventually I loosened my grip on any semblance of a career and advancement. By 2001, I had resigned and spent most days pouring over medical journals and keeping close tabs on Sue.

She took my presence in stride, but I knew it must not have been easy for her to have Mommy around all the time. I'd like to think that she was grateful for the time I spent at her side, pulling her along through those first few years. And while she never told me, I feel it meant a lot to her, me being there.

It was then I inadvertently began to loiter at the Colmer-Rich Cardiology Clinic where Dr. Norris kept his office. Even on days when Sue wasn't scheduled for an appointment, I would find myself calling or dropping into the office filled with questions and literature on alternative medicine, experimental drugs, effective studies that resulted in patient improvement.

I had become obsessed with Sue's illness and, even after we relented and let her return to school to live her life again, I would still wake up with a gnawing feeling there was some small detail we were missing that could fix her.

Don on the other hand seemed far less concerned with the medical side of things and often spent his time idly chatting with Sue or cooking up fancy meals the two of them saw on the cooking shows she was always watching. It kind of annoyed me that he wasn't as concerned as I was.

In hindsight, Don was merely making up for lost time with Sue, eager to show her how much he loved her while she was still with us. I, on the other hand, wasn't ready for her to leave so I constantly looked for something to keep her around longer.

One night, after Sue had moved to Boston, I was tossing and turning. Eventually I got up, dressed, and wandered to the study where I lazily thumbed through a textbook called *Heart Disease: Environment, Stress and Gender.* The medical journals were piled quite high by this point.

I spent the wee hours of the morning jotting down notes and questions before heading back up-stairs to shower and get dressed. I wanted to compare assertions with Dr. Norris on a few studies contained within, so I worked up a cup of coffee and read quietly, waiting patiently for the office to open.

When I arrived at the office, I made sure to promptly sign in for a walk-up appointment as was customary for me at the time. The shrewd old lady be-hind the counter simply nodded at me as I approached the counter. Her beady eyes locked onto the sign in sheet.

I took my seat on one of the worn-out beige chairs that littered the waiting room and pulled out my notes, tucked gingerly into the textbook I had brought along for reference. After a few minutes, I was once again fully immersed in a section about macho atti-tudes and how they relate to coping in patients with cardiovascular diseases.

As I was reading, a voice rained down on me, "I like your book."

I looked up to find the same dull red textbook cover mirroring perfectly the one I was reading. It was sticking out under the arm of a tall and slender man wearing a lab coat. He was handsome and extended a crooked smile at me.

"Thank you, um, Doctor? I don't believe we've met."

"I'm Doctor Simpson. Allen. I just joined the practice last week. Are we seeing you today?"

"Oh my, no," I spoke hurriedly. "My daughter is the patient, but I'm here to grill Dr. Norris on a few things that I read in this book.

Dr. Simpson's face wrinkled into a pucker. "Well Miss, I'm afraid Dr. Norris won't be in today."

My face twisted in disappointment until I found myself gathering my things. "Right, I see," I said.

"Well, if you don't mind, I have a few minutes before my first appointment and I have read the book, so why don't you come back to my office and we can chat."

"I don't want to be a bother." As I said this we made eye-contact. It made my insides tingle. His sharp features cast shadows on his neck.

"Really, it's no bother." He reached out his hand and I took it in mine.

"Jackie. Anderson."

"Please, right this way Jackie."

Before I knew it, we were sitting in his tiny office knee to knee comparing the notes we had made in the captions of the book. As Dr. Simpson leaned over my textbook to point at a particularly interesting passage, I could smell a peculiar scent. Something between powdered donuts and Vaseline. At first I was put off by it, but the longer we sat, the more my heart fluttered.

He was bright and calming. By the time he realized he was fifteen minutes late to his first appointment of the day, he had put my mind at ease about Sue's heart. I was only with him for maybe twenty minutes, but for the rest of the day I could think of nothing else.

Don returned from a business trip that night and, feeling the guilt of my own thoughts for Allen, I offered him a nice dinner out to catch up. I craved love and attention. I wanted nothing more than to forget about my daughter for a moment and fall into the arms of the man I loved.

Don didn't pick up my desire and politely declined dinner to catch up on bills and other household chores. I didn't argue; I merely slinked up to the bedroom to read. Later, I could hear Don laughing. I snuck down the stairs and listened to him talking to Sue on the phone for thirty minutes. I started to cry.

If only he had the same amount of love for me he had for our daughters, I thought. Of course it was misguided, I wasn't really mad at him. In the moment though, I was angry and had no real outlet that wouldn't attract Don's attention or start a senseless fight. I opted for two Ambien before I buried myself in bed for the night.

The next morning, I awoke to find Don's arm draped casually around mine. I expected to relish his touch, but the intense feeling from the night before had all but vanished. We coasted through breakfast and Don was once again off to work.

Before too long, I found myself calling the Colmer-Rich Clinic and asking for Dr. Simpson. I don't think I even knew what to say.

"Hello, this is Dr. Simpson."

"Hi, yes, Doctor Simpson. It's Jackie Anderson, from yesterday."

"Well hello, Jackie! How are you this fine, fine morning?"

His voice instantly calmed me down. I slumped down into a recliner and wrapped myself in a blanket. I could feel tears welling up in my eyes. My first instinct was to tell him I didn't think my husband loved me anymore and I could think of nothing but him, instead it came out differently. "Well Doctor..."

"Please, call me Allen."

"Alright." My voice slightly increased in pitch. "Allen. I'm sorry to bother you, but after we talked yesterday, I can't shake the feeling that there's something Sue is missing, something that she might be able to try before she makes the move to a septal myectomy."

"Jackie, the best thing you can do is to relax. Sue is a bright girl. I took a look at her charts after we spoke and, according to the data, she is already doing more than most to help control her condition. While nothing is guaranteed, you must keep faith that we will do all we can for her."

"Oh Allen, I didn't mean to insinuate that you weren't. I am so sorry."

"Jackie, listen, why don't you have dinner with me tonight? I have a few books I can recommend for coping and living with cardiomyopathy. I think it's important that you stay positive and not forget to live your own life. Sue wouldn't want you wasting away yourself."

At first I was in shock. I nodded my head as I stared off into the space between me and the other side of the living room. Was he coming onto me? I wanted to see him. I began imagining him and I in the same romantic restaurant I wanted to take Don to the night before.

"That...that sounds lovely." It came out of my mouth before I could do anything about it.

"My last appointment is at five-fifteen, so maybe an hour after that would work? We can meet at Carlotta's. Do you know it?"

"Of course."

And that was all it took to begin my affair with Doctor Allen Simpson. That first night we did indeed have dinner, a simple Italian bistro filled with wine and pleasant conversation. And he did bring me two books, one titled *Heart Sense for Women* and the other one called, *Thriving with Heart Disease*. I was grateful for the company and the books. So grateful that at the end of the night, I kissed Dr. Simpson clean on the mouth.

Then after the jolt of the moment, I led him to my car and kissed him in the back seat like a high school girl fawning over the captain of the football team. It was wrong, it was maybe a little dirty, but it made me feel something powerful for the first time in years.

While we kissed, we said very little. His strong hands searched my body for more, but before it went too far, I stopped him. I straightened my blouse and hair and we agreed to meet again that weekend.

This began a long and tenuous love affair between myself and the good doctor. We would meet at bars or at his office, eventually moving past kissing to sex in quiet motels or on the desk at his office very late at night.

It all felt surreal, and never conventional or nearly as romantic as I expected an affair to feel. We never went to his place and I didn't dare allow him into my home, where my family was still very much intact.

The girls had moved out of the house by this time and it was very quiet around the house—almost too quiet, with Don working so often. It gave me anxiety to be there alone most days.

I knew what I was doing wasn't right, but something about being with Allen was soothing. My fears over Sue lessened when I was with him.

Sue was still fighting to stay alive and I think, in my mind, that was my way of rationalizing my affair with Allen. I told myself that this was helping, to be so close to a doctor, and before I knew it, three years had gone by.

I never loved him. I doubt he loved me, but that connection, his gentle touch brought me out of my funk and helped me enjoy life in a way Don was no longer capable of. I still loved Don, but he was increasingly distant as the years passed. I told myself he was cheating on me too; it helped me sleep when the Ambien didn't.

All the same, Allen was sweet. He would bring me treats like gourmet chocolates or bottles of rare wine. He certainly played the part of suitor, even if he never intended to commit completely. I think this is why I kept up with the affair for so long. It was like a warm bath. Eventually, we even fell into a routine that suited us both. Thursday afternoons and Monday mornings were *our time* with the occasional night out when Don was on a business trip.

Our time usually consisted of thunderous sex wherever was convenient followed by a bite to eat or a discussion about whatever study either of us had come across that week concerning Sue's condition. Looking back, it was very regimented and formal in a way.

One would think, in all that time thinking and talking about it, we would have come up with a suitable solution for her heart disease, but we never did. It was merely a thin thread that kept driving me back into his arms.

At first, I craved my time with Allen. I would count the hours until I could see him. I was selfish and thought this was the only way I could cope. Then after some time, I didn't crave it as much, but I was afraid of going back to the life I had before. I didn't want to be in constant fear of losing Sue or be alone in our big house.

Allen was a comfort both physically and emotionally. Whether he knew it or not, I needed him, even if it was still just a kinky little secret a few times a week. Of course, this came crashing down after a re-markable eight years of sneaking around.

It was a Monday and I was driving Allen back to the clinic. It wasn't uncommon for me to quickly pick him up and drive us to a coffee shop or a motel for a few hours. It never stopped feeling a bit dirty and childish, but when I was with him, he had a wonder-fully calming effect on me.

I pulled up to the curb to drop him off and leaned in for a kiss, "Have a wonderful afternoon." Our lips pressed firmly together. I remember the radio was playing a Carly Simon song, *Nobody Does It Better*.

He stepped out of the car and onto the sidewalk, I watched him brush past a young woman and head into the building. I followed him with my eyes until he was out of sight and as I was about to put my car in drive and head home, I realized the young woman was still frozen on the sidewalk.

It was Sue. Her face was twisted as if she had been sprayed with mace. I stared at her through my windshield, mortified. She stood there staring at me too, and it was agonizing. Eventually I jumped out of the car and said, "Sue! Please, let me explain."

It was a phrase I had heard a hundred times on the romance movie of the week. But I had no good explanation for my actions, let alone anything reason-able I could tell my daughter so she wouldn't hate me. I was caught red-handed, but I still didn't want to dis-appoint her.

"Does Dad know?" was all Sue could manage through her trembling voice. Her eyes darted around the parking lot, as if she was searching for her father to help make sense of it all.

"Sue, get in the car, please. Let's talk," I said.

I half expected her to take off running, only to later find her under an old wild oak tree in the park, devastated at her broken family and evil mother. But, instead, she simply took a deep breath and calmly got into the passenger side of my car. I quickly joined her in the car.

"I don't want to scream at you here, but what the hell is going on, Mom? Drive, just drive."

I didn't say a word. I threw the car into drive and sped off. I had no excuses for my behavior. She had no reason to believe Allen was a comfort to me, something her father had neglected to be ever since she was first sick.

"I don't love him. It's...hard to explain," I started.

Sue buried her face in her hands. "Mom, how could you? And with one of my doctors! This is...I don't know what to do."

"First of all, he isn't one of your doctors." The words fell out and immediately felt wrong. "Sweetheart, please, you can't tell your father! It's not good for your heart."

I was grasping at straws. Of course it all felt like self-preservation at that point, but there wasn't much else I could do.

"I suppose you know right? You are the one fucking a cardiologist."

"Okay, I deserve that. You have to believe me, I didn't mean for it to happen. We weren't together in the beginning. It just happened."

"When? When did it start?"

I continued to drive aimlessly, thinking of the best way to answer the question sent a small tinge of pain to my temple. "Honey, it's been awhile. Your father...I needed something to keep me from worrying about you all the time."

"Oh so this is my fault?" Sue said.

I began to cry, "No! That isn't what I meant. It was after you got sick, your father stopped being with me and started being with you. I didn't know what to do! I read a lot, you know that. I studied and spent a lot of time at Dr. Norris' office and Allen was a huge help..."

"Allen? Oh God. You are fucking a guy named Allen?"

"Language, honey, please."

"Mom, stop it."

"Can we talk about what are you doing in town? Why were you at Dr. Norris' office? Why didn't you call me? Is everything alright?"

Sue took a deep breath, almost as if she too was hiding a secret on the same level as my infidelity.

"I didn't want to say anything until I was sure. Last week during a routine echo my ejection fraction was twenty-five percent. Needless to say, it was enough to warrant a reevaluation of my treatment."

"Oh my God, Sue."

"Mom, calm down. We measured it today and it was back up around forty-five. Dr. Norris thinks it might have been a warning sign, and that I need to think about an ICD."

My hands started to tremble and I was feeling queasy. A defibrillator implanted into my little girl's chest? I could feel my own heart beating like butterfly wings. I slowed the car down slightly so I could turn to look at my daughter. Her eyes were red and she clearly was completely overwhelmed.

"I'm so sorry. You have so much to think about already and now to top it off, your slut of a mom got caught cheating on your father."

She took a deep breath. "I didn't think that was who you were. I feel like I don't know anything about you. Why?" She sniffed and then wrinkled her face up as she began to sob.

I put my hand on her knee and she quickly jerked her leg away. I had betrayed both Sue and her father. I started to cry again.

"No! You don't get to cry. You screwed up, take ownership of that. You're going to tell Sam and Dad or I'm going to do it for you. It's not right, it's not okay. You owe that to them."

"Honey, sometimes people grow apart," I pleaded with her. "Your father and I have been going down this path for a while. I love him, but it just isn't the same. Allen and I...it's not love, but he gives me attention and helps me keep my mind off of your heart disease. I needed that in my life and your father wasn't giving it to me. It's not an excuse, it's the truth. Please forgive me."

I continued to drive, though at this point I wasn't sure if I should drive toward our house. I would risk Don being home and having to throw Sue in the middle of all this. I considered looking for a cliff to drive off of to avoid confrontation. Either way, I was in the weeds and suffocating.

The car was silent then. Sue had controlled her emotions and neither of us was crying as much anymore. We were done talking for the time being and the air was full of tension. Tension that I was solely responsible for.

What was I going to do? I sensed my marriage would be over and my daughters would hate me. I knew I was in the wrong, but at the same time, I wasn't sure I would have changed anything. Allen was truly a comfort whether Sue could understand that or not.

"Where am I taking you?" I asked.

At first Sue didn't say anything, she only stared out the window like a little girl pouting because I wouldn't take her for ice cream. And she was my little girl, even at twenty-nine years old.

"Back to the clinic," she said solemnly.

I diligently drove back towards Dr. Norris' office, where I had driven many times before. None of it mattered anymore.

I thought about Allen. Did this mean it was over between us? What would I tell him? If Don left me, would Allen take me in? Would he even care? Would I even want that?

He shared in this despicable act and if I was really being honest with myself, he was worse. He knew I was married, knew I was vulnerable and still let it all happen. I wanted it, but he made it so easy to lose my way.

I considered this for a moment and then for the first time since my affair started, I felt like a whore. I was cheating on a wonderful person with a man that didn't love me and didn't care I was married. What had I done?

We continued to drive without a word until we passed Sticky Pete's. It was a BBQ place Don and I had frequented when we were younger. We had taken the girls there a few times in an attempt to recapture our youth, and they fell in love too.

Sue sighed and muttered something under her breath.

"What was that?" I asked. I was nervous and surprised she spoke at all.

"Sticky Pete's. I haven't been there in ages," Sue said.

"It's wonderful, isn't it?" I asked.

Sue still faced the window and made no effort to directly address me.

I continued, "I could eat if you could."

"Mom. Stop. Do you really think Sticky Pete is going to fix all of this?" She cracked a smile.

"I bet you never thought you would ever say that sentence?"

It didn't matter, nothing was going to fix the mess I made. I wasn't sure why I turned the car around and pulled into the parking lot of Sticky Pete's, but it was my last ditch effort to keep my daughter.

"For old time's sake?" I said. She considered the proposition in front of her. Sticky Pete was a powerful olive branch.

"Okay, fine. But I can only have one bite of their cinnamon rolls, I shouldn't have sweets."

And with that we headed inside to Sticky Pete's. It was before lunch and we quickly settled into a booth with faded orange vinyl. It squeaked and buckled as we slid into our seats.

The room around us was busy with activity and the sweet smell of smoked meat filled the air. Everyone was involved in their own worlds, so it felt safe sitting there with Sue.

I was truly sad, and when I got sad I wanted to eat. Sticky Pete wouldn't know what hit him. I began imagining all of the things I was going to order, a drink was top of mind.

"This doesn't change anything," Sue said as she browsed the menu.

"Sue, what can I do?"

"Tell Dad," she said firmly.

"He'll leave me!" I noticed I was subconsciously squeezing my thumb and forefinger together quite hard. When I released them, my whole hand quivered.

"Nobody wants that, but it's his choice to make and his alone. And honestly, I'm going to support his decision. I know you didn't think this through, but you cheated on your husband, so you really don't have much of a leg to stand on. Dammit, it just makes me angry to think about it! Don't you care about him at all?"

Her voice was cold. She wasn't giving me an inch. I supposed the fact she was there sitting in the booth with me was a sign she wasn't going to disown me, but I could see the disappointment in her face. If she ever looked up to me before, it was long gone.

And what would Sam think when I told her? And Don? He almost certainly would leave me. He was sensitive and proud. Maybe we had grown apart, but that didn't excuse my behavior. This wasn't the first time I imagined what Don would do if he found out about me and Allen, but it was first time I knew I would have to tell him.

The waitress came to take our order. The smile on her face directly conflicted with the demeanor of our table. We ordered two chicken sandwiches with potato salad on the side and a single world-famous Sticky Pete roll. When the waitress crossed the room to fetch us two glasses of water, Sue began rapping the table with her fingernails.

"Sue," I said, "can you ever forgive me?"

"It's a little fresh don't you think? I feel like this is all my fault. If I never got sick, you and Dad never would have...and you wouldn't have felt so lonely. How did this happen? This wasn't supposed to happen."

"You really want to know?"

"No Mother, I don't want to know the sordid details of your affair. It would probably be bullshit anyway. This is a perfect example of why I've removed love from my life!"

"Please keep your voice down. I get it. I messed up. I guess I've been messing up for a very long time. Sometimes people get lost, can't you understand that?"

As I looked at Sue, begging for a response, I found it in her eyes. She looked down to her lap and fell silent. I knew she was worried about her health, her life and I was only piling on.

"Mom, when I first was diagnosed I told myself I would never let myself fall in love. I didn't want to put anyone through it, to experience losing me. I haven't allowed myself to have a boyfriend since college. I don't want that person to feel loss when I finally go. But I found love last year. I met this guy and slept with him right away. Then I ran away and didn't allow him to pursue me. It was the hardest thing I've ever done. But I didn't want to hurt him. I was trying to protect him from feeling betrayed and lost. That's how Dad is going to feel."

She cleared her throat and started to continue, but our food had arrived. She took a deep breath and dove into the cinnamon roll first. I smiled when she wasn't looking and put a napkin in my lap. After we were settled and the waitress had wandered off, she continued.

"I've been very lonely. Maybe you do need someone to support you and be there for you, even in the worst of times. I guess I always thought that person for you was Dad. And if what you're telling me is true, that he hasn't been there for you, well I'm sorry for you. We all should have a person to go to when times are hard. But did you even talk to him about it, first? Tell me you tried as hard as you could before you went to...that other guy."

Sue then reached her fork out and pulled off a generous portion of cinnamon roll and shoved it in her mouth before I could argue with her. She was right, of course she was.

Sue then reached for another bite but before her fork could make contact with the sticky goodness of the cinnamon roll, I calmly pulled the plate back towards me.

"You already had two bites dear." I glared at her, challenging her to argue. But she didn't, she nodded knowingly and lowered her fork.

We spent the rest of the lunch eating quietly and when we were finished I paid without any objections from Sue and we headed back to the car.

"You want me to take you to your car?"

"Yeah, I have to drive the three hours, so I better get a move on."

I drove her to the office hoping that Allen didn't see us. He was the last person I wanted to see now. When we got to the parking lot, I pulled into a spot on the side furthest from the entrance.

Sue gathered her things and pulled the door open, then without looking at me she said, "Mom, I still love you." She got out and wandered off to find her car.

I sat there for a moment, not sure of what to do. She didn't remind me to tell Don about my infidelity, though I knew she would be expecting me to tell him.

My hands felt clammy as I put the car into drive. I pulled out of the parking lot and turned left towards home. Don would be home in a few hours and I decided he needed to know immediately, like a Band-Aid that needed to come off. He would, of course, be devastated.

I wondered as I drove home whether or not I would have willingly confessed to Don had Sue not caught me. It had been eight long years, but maybe I would have quit on my own and kept it to myself. I don't think I ever felt truly bad about what I was doing. I supposed I thought I was somehow helping Sue by befriending Allen.

I drove into the garage, came inside the house and settled myself onto our couch with a glass of wine and a pen and paper. I was considering writing Don a letter, but no words came to me as I sat there. After some time, I must have fallen asleep because the next thing I knew I was being gently shaken awake.

I opened my eyes and came face to face with my darling husband Don, who had knelt down to my level on the couch. He had a big smile on his face and I immediately began to cry.

"Jackie? What's wrong honey?" Don said.

My eyes filled with tears and through the wet blur I could see the concern growing on his face. He really was a good man and I had to let him down.

"Don, I owe you an apology. I haven't been faithful to you," I said.

Don slumped down to both knees on the floor at my words.

"I don't understand. You cheated on me?"

He looked as though I had taken the wind out of him. He put his hands up to his temples trying to comprehend what I was telling him.

I thought I was prepared, or that I had the right words to say to him, but watching him try to piece it together, all I could do was nod.

Suddenly he reached out and grabbed my wrist hard.

"You had sex with someone else?" He was asking the same question, just using different words. His grip tightened and his eyes were watering.

"Don, stand up, please," my lip quivered, "don't be the victim. What I did is inexcusable, I hurt the man I loved. I'm the evil one. I need you to be angry, I need you to scream at me."

"Jackie? What is going on? You don't love me anymore?"

He looked lost, genuinely hurt. I did this to him. He was still on his knees, his face white as he stared me down.

"You aren't listening to me! I cheated on you! I screwed someone else. I did the worst thing I could possibly do to you. I ruined us."

"Were you trying to hurt me? Did you do this to get back at me for something?" He let go of my wrists and let his hands fall into his lap.

I rubbed my wrist and fell back deeper into the sofa, "No dear. I thought I was missing something and I was looking for it anywhere that made sense. I messed up. I needed you, and you weren't there."

"So this is my fault? I did this? No, no, you never once told me that you weren't happy. How can I fix something that I don't know is broken?"

He was right. I never gave him a chance to fight for me, to be the man I needed him to be. I reached for his hands, but he folded his arms across this chest and stood up.

"How long?"

"What do you mean?"

"How long has this been going on? Was it only one time?"

"No."

"How long?"

I didn't want to tell him, I stared at the wall. This would crush him. Then the words just came out, "eight years..."

"Eight...Jackie, are you fucking serious?"

Again I could only manage to nod my head. The tears were coming down my cheeks in sheets now. I watched as he ran both of his hands through his hair, turned and left the room. I called after him, but it was no use. He was leaving and there was nothing I could do about it.

CHAPTER TEN
Donald 2010

You aren't supposed to outlive your children, that much I know. This fact alone left me ill equipped to properly deal with the news that my daughter had cardiomyopathy. Truth be told, short of my general worries about a heart attack, I didn't have much knowledge of heart disease, let alone the kind of heart disease that strikes pretty young eighteen-year-olds.

All I knew was my time on this earth with Sue was cut down. None of us really knew how long she actually had, but I'll be damned if I wasn't going to take full advantage of it. She was my little girl. She was my first child and not to put my other daughter Sam down, but Sue and I had a magic connection.

When my wife Jackie and I found out we were pregnant, she was very clear she wanted a girl. I wasn't the type of father to really care one way or the other about the sex of the baby. As we got closer to the due date I had convinced myself that we were having a boy. I had dreams about it, it felt right.

So when little Sue popped out, with her wavy red hair, pudgy face and what was clearly a vagina, I was initially in shock. Not because she was a beautiful baby girl. No, I was upset because I was wrong. And that is pretty much how life has gone for me ever since.

I figured I would have two wonderful kids who would make me proud and live long amazing lives. The first part was certainly coming true, but the second part was threatening to fall short for Sue.

Almost immediately after we found out what we were dealing with, I began spending as much time seeing and talking with my daughter. I didn't want to have any regrets about the little time I did have with her. I showered her with gifts, took her to fancy restaurants and most importantly took her on the greatest trip of our lives.

Shortly after my wife confessed she had been cheating on me with one of Sue's Doctors, I had no choice but to file for divorce. The situation was regrettable all around and I'd be lying if I said I didn't see it coming. I knew my focus had shifted from my wife to my daughter over the years, but it still stung.

While the divorce was progressing, I drove up to visit Sue. She wasn't in the best of places during this time. Her heart was acting up and she had convinced herself she wouldn't be around by next Christmas.

The prospect of losing my wife and my daughter in such a short amount of time was almost more than I could handle. What I needed was an escape.

I pulled up to her apartment complex and parked facing the setting sun. It was a bright clear day and there were the kinds of clouds you could lay in the grass watching them take on different shapes.

One of the clouds looked like an elephant. Elephants were traditionally painted as wise and majestic creatures, and at the time I was feeling very much the opposite. Maybe what I needed was to commune with them. It gave me an idea.

I made my way up to her apartment door and as I was about to knock, she pulled the door open. It was a game we played when we met up. We would watch for each other and try to answer the door before the other knocked.

The look on her face was of pure joy. I knew she had been depressed, she told me as much, but standing there I saw her forget about all her troubles and enjoy herself. I stepped into the doorway and gave her the biggest hug I could muster.

Later as we sat down for dinner, I pushed my asparagus back and forth on the plate and I thought out loud.

"Sue, we should go on a trip."

"Where to?"

"Somewhere big."

"Like the world's largest ball of twine or something?"

"No, come on, somewhere big, somewhere you've always wanted to go. Think of it like a bucket list thing. What about Africa? Didn't you always beg me to go?" I looked up to the ceiling to express the size of the statement. It was at that moment I knew we had to do it. It wasn't just about Sue, it was about me and her taking flight and starting fresh.

"Africa!" Her eyes lit up like the sunrise on an ocean. She cocked her head and stared at me for a moment intently.

"I'm serious Sue. You want to go to Africa, let's go to Africa and ride elephants and eat monkey brains." I took a large swill from my iced tea and slammed it down on the table.

"I don't think they eat monkeys anymore, Dad."

"Let's go on safari and race cheetahs! Let's go while we're still young!"

"You're really serious, Dad?" Sue was beginning to understand the weight of the conversation.

"I am honey. I need to get out of this place for a while. You need to experience life. Why not? Why not pack up and spend a few weeks out in the world? I've gotta shake my shitty reality."

"What if something happens, you know, while we're out there?" her voice wavered.

"What if we stay here and never know what it's like to watch a lion run down a gazelle or never get to see where all the t-shirts go that are printed up for the losers of the Super Bowl?"

Sue slumped in her chair for a moment thinking. You could see the excitement rise and fall on her face as she considered what I was offering. "Okay Daddy, I'll bite. Let's do it!"

So, there we were seventeen days later, climbing aboard a stretched Land Rover headed for the Ngorongoro Conservation Area outside of the Serengeti National Park in Tanzania. We were ready for safari. We were ready for the trip of a lifetime.

My other daughter Sam couldn't make the trip because of a recent deployment, so it was Sue and me. Her in her big floppy straw hat and me in my cargo pants with twenty-seven pockets.

We began the trip driving through the countryside for three hours from the Arusha Airport. The country was gorgeous and flat. This allowed us to see for miles and hypothesize what lay at the brink of our vision.

The driver, who was coarse and brash at first, soon warmed up to my daughter as she politely asked him about the photo of his children pinned neatly on his sun visor. He was so pleased with her that he excitedly pointed out landmarks on the plains as we drove.

Eventually, we descended on our first destination, the Ngorongoro Sopa Lodge outside of the great crater of Ngorongoro. The lodge was not as rustic as I was hoping; I wanted to rough it and experience Africa like the natives did so long ago. Sue, on the other hand, had no reservations with the fact there was a pool that overlooked the caldera and a continental breakfast.

Early the next morning we were picked up from the lodge by a young man named Rama who was to be our guide on a wildlife tour of the crater. Rama moved slowly, almost as majestically as the animals we were intending to see that day. He reminded me a bit of myself at his age. His muscles were showing through his thin-and worn-down Kansas City Royals t-shirt. Rama and I became instant friends. He was lively and helped put Sue's suburban nerves to bed.

The sun was beginning to rise as Rama, Sue and I drove to another lodge to pick up a pair who would be joining us on Safari. Alec and Brittany Tennison were newlyweds from England. They could have been mistaken for Siamese twins had they not independently climbed into the SUV.

Sue rolled her eyes slightly as they gripped each other's khaki-covered arms with each bump and rumble of the road. They said very little throughout the day, only managing to whisper and baby talk each other when they thought no one was listening.

Rama started the group off easy as we passed near a small body of water filled with wild flamingos. It was a good chance to climb out of the truck to go over the rules of the day and to snap a few photos with a gorgeous pink background.

"Listen, everyone, please," Rama said, "Today we'll see lots of beautiful animals and creatures of Africa. Some dangerous, and some, like the flamingo, not so much. I ask when I give you a direction while animals are near, you listen please."

Rama was standing on the hood of the Land Rover as he spoke, his dark skin drawing in the sun. "Everyone duck!" Rama yelled and covered his face with his arms. My first instinct was to look around for impending danger. Sue and the Tennisons screamed and dropped to the ground like children.

By the time I had made a full circle and focused my gaze back on the truck, Rama was laughing hysterically. I joined him as he helped Sue off the ground.

"Sue? I thought you were my strong and resilient daughter? Just because your Daddy is here doesn't mean you have to pretend to be a helpless little girl!"

She dusted off her jacket and adjusted the floppy hat on her head. "Shut up. I was just following directions!"

"Well dear, you've always been good at that," I smirked and patted her on the back. I used to think she was fragile and delicate, but over time I learned she could be as thick-skinned when she wanted to be. She wasn't going to let anything stop her.

The group gathered back inside the truck as Rama told us, "From here on out, we stay in the truck. We'll get out briefly at lunch, but the beasts will eat you if you get out too soon." He chuckled to himself and the rest of the group looked uneasy.

It was one thing to act tough around flamingos, but we were headed out to see the biggest creatures in the animal kingdom. We were looking for rhinos and lions.

Things could get interesting in a hurry.

Whether she knew it or not, Sue had slowly scooted closer and closer to me on the bench we were sitting on as we drove. I didn't mind at all, as this was exactly why we took the trip in the first place: to bond. It was nice to be there and sharing the experience with her. It's something I could take with me for the rest of my life.

"So, talked to your mother much?" I said, trying to make casual conversation over the rumble of the tires gliding effortlessly over the dirt road.

Sue turned and looked me hard in the face. "Why on Earth would you want to know that?"

I suddenly felt like she was towering over me as I shrunk deeper into my seat. "Cut me some slack, kid. Your mother and I were together for a very long time. Part of me, I don't know, still cares a little. Even if she is a jerk..."

Sue scoffed and Rama looked through the rearview mirror, "Having a good time, Don?"

"You have no idea, Rama!" I took a deep breath and looked out the open window. The plains moved past us in an almost mocking way. The grass leaned far away from the road as we made our way deeper into the crater.

I looked over at the Tennisons, who gave me polite smiles before turning back towards the window and their secret love whispers.

"So?" I said.

"So what?" Sue said.

"How is your Mother?"

Sue shrugged, "I haven't really spoken to her. She tried to call me a few times before we left, but I'm not ready to answer."

"Sue, please, she's still your Mother. Don't punish her for what she did. That's my job. You know how much it means to her to be connected to you. She's still a good person deep down. She, well, lost her way a little. You shouldn't alienate her for it."

"So I am supposed to forgive her? Are we all going to be best buddies?"

"Well first off, we are family, so we don't have to be best friends. And hell no, I'm not forgiving her. She screwed me over, literally. I'm going to need a lot of time and a lot of bourbon to understand that. I doubt very much it had anything to do with me and if it did I can only imagine I deserved it. Either way, I still love her in a lot of ways. Even if I curse her from my tiny apartment."

She snuggled into my arm and squeezed me tightly. I knew she was taking my side in the matter, but it still made me feel a little guilty. When Sue was growing up, she always told her poor Mother she hated her and loved Daddy best. At that point, sitting there with Sue on an African Safari, I couldn't disagree with that.

The truck rumbled on, driving further and further into the caldera. Rama explained the history of the area, including Zinjanthropus, the earliest known human remains found in the world.

"This is where life began. That's a comforting thought," Sue whispered almost to herself.

We passed a large group of eland grazing to our left, the first real sign of substantial wildlife. They looked up once the truck got close enough, but evidently didn't see us as much of a threat because they stood firm in place, casually watching us pass by.

We continued to see large groups of gazelle, ze-
bra, and wildebeest in short bursts, but Rama told us
today we were looking for the elusive black rhinoceros, of which there were only around twenty or so in
the crater. It became the goal for the day. Find a rhino.

"The female rhinos stay together with their
calves in what we call a crash," Rama told us as we
drove, "It's the males who wander off on their own."

"A crash?" One of the Tennison twins chimed in.

"It's another word for a grouping, like a congress
of salamanders," Sue said.

Several times, off in the distance, we thought we
saw a rhino and begged Rama to change directions,
only to discover a boulder or a bush instead. It was
exciting and terrifying at the same time. We certainly
were feeling like intruders as we passed by one herd of
animals after another.

Eventually we stopped for lunch, still without so
much as a glimpse of the rhino. We did, however, welcome the chance to get out of the truck and stretch our
legs.

Rama had neatly packed a small cooler with water, cold chicken, boiled eggs, some carrots and cel-
ery. He unwrapped everything delicately and passed it
around for the group. The spread was a welcome sight
in the heat of midday. We settled on a small ring of
logs that must have been set up specifically for these
safari lunches and started to eat.

"Rama?" I said.

"Yes, my friend?"

"Is it safe to sleep out here at night?"

"Oh yes! The best night of sleep you can ever have. Of course the park has dedicated camping areas now."

"To protect folks from the lions?"

"Protecting the animals from us. This is a delicate and beautiful place. We'll keep it that way."

"Excellent point," Sue said. Alec and Brittany nodded in agreement as they chewed their chicken in unison. As we ate, a small group of water buffalo meandered nearby. We couldn't have asked for a more gratifying spot to stop for lunch.

The buffalo and truck were positioned near one of the few trees in the immediate vicinity, so I suspected they were in search of shade, like we were. It was comforting in a way, almost as if they were accepting us as equals in their home. I leaned back and in the moment felt like a huge weight was lifted off of me.

"You two seem very happy," I said to the Tennisons. "How long have you been together?"

Brittany covered her mouth with her hand as she finished chewing up a piece of hard-boiled egg. She smiled and said, "two years, but we got married a week past."

"That's sweet. I just left my wife. She's been cheating on me for several years and we're getting divorced."

Sue smacked me hard on the arm. "Dad!"

"All I'm saying is that even amongst pain and suffering, happiness is still possible. They're happy.

That could be you." I motioned to the mortified Tennisons.

"I have to apologize for my father," Sue said. Their looks of shock and anguish were growing.

"He's having a truly defining moment in life. Really, we're so happy for you. You make a lovely couple," She smiled the way only Sue knew how and turned to me with a whisper, "Oh. My. God. Dad. Could you be more awkward?"

"Sorry," I mumbled and stuffed the rest of my lunch into my mouth without saying another word. As we were packing our trash back into the cooler, the group of water buffalo wandered closer to the truck. The Tennisons decided it would be a good opportunity to get up close and personal with Africa.

With Rama's back turned, Alec inched closer to the nearest buffalo while his wife framed the shot in her camera. The buffalo peacefully chewed on the grass nearby as Alec got his picture taken.

It seemed harmless enough, so I pulled my small camera from one of the pockets in my pant leg. "Sue, your turn. Get over there," I said.

"Um, okay," Sue cautiously made her way towards the buffalo and stood awkwardly for a photo. As she got into position, a loud bang sounded in the distance. I looked up from my camera to see another truck speeding across the plain. Its muffler was bouncing wildly and another loud popping sound echoed around us.

This was enough to not only spook me, but the buffalo as well. They started to scatter in panic. Rama pulled himself out of the back of the truck to survey the chaos. Alec, Brittany and Sue started to run towards the truck, staying slightly ahead of the buffalo, which were now bearing down on our position.

I sprang into action. I was already closer to the truck than the rest of the group, so I was hoping to make it there first and open the door. As I started running in that direction, Sue screamed. I turned to see Rama grab her by the arm and thrust her to the ground as one of the water buffalo just missed them and ran head first into the side of the truck. The truck shook at the impact as Alec, Brittany and myself pushed our way inside. The three of us were thrown across the inside of the truck. My elbow smashed into Alec and I grabbed Brittany to keep her from getting lost underneath the bench.

The buffalo pushed against the truck a few times before a loud whistle sounded. Rama had jumped onto the hood of the truck, as he had earlier in the morning. He was waving his arms frantically and blowing on an old wooden reed. When he finished, I watched as the remaining buffalo scampered off into the distance.

"Sue? Are you okay?" I shouted. I heard nothing. My mind started racing. Those beasts were so big, it wouldn't have taken much to do some damage. I charged out the still open door of the truck and practically skid across the dirt ground towards the back.

The side of the truck was crumbled to the point that I wondered if the door would ever shut again.

A million thoughts cropped up and it seemed to take a lifetime to go the few feet to the other side of the truck. We were in the middle of nowhere. I prayed she wasn't seriously hurt or worse.

When I turned past the edge of the truck, I found Sue sitting with her back leaning against the tailgate and her knees up in front of her. With her right hand, she clutched her shirt, as if it was too tight. Her left hand lay face up in the dirt, lifeless. The sun was directly above us and reflected off of sheen of the bumper in a burst of light.

I could no longer see her clearly as the sun splashed onto my face. "Sue?" I called again. I could tell she didn't move to look up at me. To my left I could see Rama several yards away, waving and clapping his hands at the few remaining buffalo that had lost steam and were making their way back towards our position.

"Please God, don't do this." I said it out loud, but it was meant to be to myself. I threw myself to the ground and grabbed her chin, pulling her face up to mine. It was then I was certain she had passed out.

I pulled her into me and began to rock her like a baby. Not here, not now, I thought.

"It's okay, sweetie. Calm down now. Everything is fine." But I was having a hard time listening to my own advice. There was nothing but dirt and sky as far as the eye could see. I started to do the math in my head. How many miles until we reached the parameter of the park? How long it would take to get to a doctor?

I was trying to convince myself that she had a chance. I stroked her hair as I continued to talk to her limp body, wondering if this would be our last moment together. "Talk to me sweetie. Tell me you're okay. I love you. Please be okay."

As I spoke, all I could think about was Gilbert O'Sullivan. Her body slack in my arms, and I was likening it to a pop song. I squeezed her tightly. When I did this, her legs pushed out and I watched as they flopped limp into the dirt below us.

I wanted to cry out, but I doubted anyone in our humble little safari could be of any help. We would never make it to any who could save her in time. My first-born was fading away before me.

I could feel my eyes beginning to water. I told her I loved her and stroked her cheek with my thumb. Then I saw her lips part and felt her chest rising. I immediately propped her upright against the truck and cradled her face in my palms.

"Sweetie? Are you there?"

Without opening her eyes, she nodded. She was regaining control! I was relieved as she turned and looked up at my face in a mixture of fear and relief. Then she smiled ever so slightly before slumping down until she was on her side, on the ground, with her face pointing to the majestic blue sky above.

I started to panic again. What was a glimmer of hope rapidly faded and I grabbed her wrist, attempting to take her pulse. My hands were shaking.

"What...are you doing?" she said.

"Sweetheart, are you okay? What happened?"

"Syncope..."

"Can you breathe? Can you sit up?" Nausea was building inside my chest when she didn't answer. I always wondered with a morbid curiosity what would be running through my head on the day my daughter died. Would I do the right thing? Would I remember to tell her how much she meant to me? Would I even have time to? Now faced with an impossible scenario, all I could think about was that damn Gilbert O'Sullivan song. I hated myself for it.

"Sue. Talk to me." I held my breath until my throat tensed up from the lack of oxygen. Finally, she spoke.

"Dad...give me a minute. I'll be fine, I need to... calm down."

As we sat there, Rama and the Tennisons gathered above us. Brittany clung to her new husband with a look of panic. I imagined it mirrored my own face. A single tear had spilled out of my eye and trickled down my face, I could feel its awkward wetness. I managed to pass a look of relief to the group.

Rama motioned to offer to help Sue up. I looked down at my daughter. Her eyes were open and darting from face to face. She still hadn't moved.

I could tell Sue was starting to feel uncomfortable, so I reach down and pulled her to her feet. At first, she was resistant, pulling back against the ground. Finally, with brute strength, I had her on her feet and tucked against my body.

"It's okay. I got the wind knocked out of me and then I blacked out."

"You said syncope. Have you been fainting like this back home?" I asked.

"Not really..." she pulled away and tried to stand on her own. Her body turned away from me as she rested again the truck.

Rama, pleased no one was seriously hurt, surveyed the damage on the truck. He slammed the door close hard a few times and it eventually caught the latch. Satisfied, he declared it, "*Que, Sera, Sera,*" and let out a soft chuckle.

The rest of us weren't sure what to do. We continued to stare at Sue as she regained the color in her face.

"I'm fine, really. Don't worry about me. I just got winded. Please let's not make a big deal about it and just keep going," she said.

So we did. Without another word, we continued the drive. It took everything in my being not to argue with Sue. I was worried. Something wasn't right, but every time I pressed her to talk to me about it, she brushed it off as nothing.

I had no choice, but to let it go and try to focus on the beauty of our surroundings. After some time, I caught a glimpse of Sue laughing at something Rama had said. That was all it took to calm me down. Before I knew it, the day was back on track and I was feeling brave. It was like we both dodged a bullet.

That day we saw a herd of giraffe, a pride of lion, even a smattering of hippos basking in the sun. It was amazing and we filled up our cameras with dazzling amateur shots. I wouldn't have traded it for the world.

Even though we never saw the black rhino, we made it back to our lodge that night elated at the wildlife we had seen. I knew coming to Africa would be memorable, but it changed me. I don't think I could have appreciated life more than I did that evening.

When we got back to the resort, I convinced Sue to take a quick nap. While she slept, I showered and dressed for dinner. It was hard to resist the urge to question Sue further about what had happened behind the truck. It worried me and I watched her carefully as we sat down to dinner that night, looking for signs of fatigue or distress.

Our table was outside and we stared at the sparkling stars in the sky, overlooking the crater we spent the afternoon in. As the waiter brought our menu, I was anxious. I watched her sip her on her water, completely at peace in the open air. Without looking up she said, "Dad. It was nothing, okay? I just got freaked out."

"What are you talking about?" I lied.

"Oh come on, I can see it in your eyes. You're worried. I wouldn't have come here with you if I didn't think I could handle it. I...got a little overwhelmed is all."

"Thank God I was here. I haven't seen you like that in a very long time. Frankly, it scared the shit out of me. And this isn't just about me. I can't always be there and you need someone around, someone who cares about you and loves..." My thoughts trailed off and I began pushed a fork around on the table, avoiding her eyes.

I could feel her watching me. I looked up to meet her gaze as she pushed her chair away from the table to leave. "Sweetheart, please stay. I didn't mean to upset you."

"You're just as bad as Mom! You think I like being alone all the time? You think I like waking up wondering if today is going to my last day on earth? Why in the world would I put that on someone else?" She sat down hard, the chair creaking under the force.

I looked at her for a moment, admiring her folded arms and furrowed brow. "Sue. Did you ever stop to think that maybe someone wants to go through that? That someone is capable of overlooking all that stuff for a chance to love a unique, beautiful, smart, and amazing woman."

I shifted in my seat to lean in closer to her, "Do you think just because you are sick that I should turn my back on you? No. I love you regardless. Don't put that on yourself. Don't let your heart disease define who you are. You're better than that. And for God's sake, don't compare your love life with mine. You can be happy. You have too damn much to offer not to be."

I took a much-needed breath and waited for my brilliant daughter to tear apart my logic and push off everything I had said. When she didn't say a word, I found myself ordering dinner and a large bourbon. We sat in silence for what seemed like eternity when she finally spoke.

"Dad, I'm really going to miss you when I die."

"Sweetie, don't talk like that."

"It's true though. You always know what to say, even when I don't want to hear it. You're right. I have let love fall to the wayside, even when I knew for sure I could be happy. I did it because I didn't want to hurt them. But it turns out I was only hurting myself."

"You still have time. There is a lot of love left in you."

"Dad? Doesn't it weird you out that you're essentially trying to talk me into having sex with someone?" She flashed a grin letting me know we were best friends again. I took a gulp of my bourbon.

"Let's try not to focus on that part, okay?" I grinned and awkwardly rolled up my napkin as the waiter arrived and laid out an amazing spread in front of us. We had every piece of fresh fruit imaginable, from mangoes and bananas to kiwis and pineapple. There was steamed rice and duck, marmalade chili and generous portions of fresh baked breads.

Once the food arrived, the conversation dropped to a simmer. We would occasionally comment on something we had seen that afternoon or run through the remaining activities left on the trip. I didn't bring up Sue's love life again. I felt like maybe she was finally on the same page as I was.

We came to Africa on a whim, putting our broken lives on hold long enough for a father and a daughter to find a secret place to fall in love with each other's company again. It served as another check on Sue's ultimate bucket list and I was thrilled beyond belief to give that to her. It was by far the best thing we could have done and it happened just in time.

I couldn't have asked for a better daughter. She never let me down and I often bragged on her to friends and co-workers. But even then, there were still nights, after her mother and I split, that I woke up in a sweat. Wondering if Sue had taken her last breath.

In my life, with all the machismo I usually carried around with me, I still got weak at the knees thinking about losing my daughter. It was bad enough Sam was in the military and could fall into tragedy at any moment herself. Mine was a life of teetering on the edge of having to deal with pain and suffering. And I had no one to grieve with me. Without Jackie, I had to do it alone.

After Africa, I devoted myself to my daughters. I talked to each of them as often as their busy lives would allow. Most of my nights were spent alone, reading or watching sports. And whenever Sam or Sue called and needed me, I was always there.

It didn't matter if they were half a world away, I would make it happen. And that is what I intend to do until the day they take their final breaths. A father shouldn't have to outlive his kid. That much I know.

CHAPTER ELEVEN
Tom 2011

I'm a self-proclaimed hopeless romantic. Believe me, that doesn't score many points with my guy friends. It's true though. I'm the guy who listens and takes note of every potential birthday or Christmas gift, even months in advance. I book trips to tiny, uncomfortable bed & breakfasts in small northeastern towns. I buy roses even when they're out of season and amazingly overpriced. If *You've Got Mail* is on TV, I can't change the channel.

I've been told I'm the quintessential nice guy. That said, I still don't know how I was able to claim Sue Anderson as my wife. She kept her last name for professional reasons so even now it's hard for me to prove she actually married me. She was a gift; I wouldn't change a single minute with her for anything or anyone.

It was happenstance we even crossed paths. It felt like a complex domino show built over weeks and weeks, only to finally go off without a hitch. But it wasn't that complicated, it was simple and real. I met Sue at a bar of all places.

When you meet someone at a bar, it becomes like a game when you talk about it with anyone else. You have to expand on the story when you tell it back. This is so you don't look too much like two people trolling a local dive bar in search of something in-between sex and a wife, kids, two dogs, and a three-car garage.

We met at a bar, though the location would turn out to be irrelevant. I was there finishing my beer after a friend had rushed home to his sick kid. It was hard not to notice her immediately and I spent some time stealing glances towards her table as I emptied my glass.

She was sitting alone, waiting. She sat there casually sipping on a water and picking at a sad salad as she checked her phone. It was kind of like a tense moment in a movie.

Once, while I was trying to get the attention of the waitress to pay my bill, we made eye contact for the briefest of moments. She smiled that polite smile when you are faced with a stranger's stare. I grinned, all lips, and quickly began staring at the wood grain in the table below me.

I'll admit, when the waitress finally came over, I ordered another beer and lingered for another chance to make eye contact again. And there we sat for at least another fifteen minutes. Both of us sitting at tables that could accommodate four people. Both alone and facing each other.

And then I saw something. I don't know if it was liquid courage or sheer boredom, but I spoke to her.

"Excuse me?" I said. She evidently didn't hear me or expect me to be addressing her, so when I first spoke to her, she didn't budge. "Is your phone new?"

I was a sucker for technology and had yet to see the latest and greatest smartphone in the flesh. It was very sexy and impressive that this girl had one before I did! I watched her as she finally looked in my direction, putting the pieces together of what I had asked her.

"Oh, uh yeah I guess so. My work gave it to me. It's supposed to be cool, right?"

I stared at her sideways, "I think you're downplaying it a bit. You know it's cool. Can I look at it?" I cautiously got out of my seat and approached her table.

She wore a sly smile on her face. "Okay, you got me, it's very cool...and shiny."

She casually passed me the phone. I turned it over in my hands a few times admiring its weight and size. I handed it back to her and she did the same thing, checking to see if I found something cool she might have initially missed.

"You're Sue Anderson, right?"

It was only after hearing her name that she looked up at me. She sighed and set her phone down before addressing me.

"Yep, that's me." She then shrugged and rolled her eyes like she thought I was going to lick her face or something. I suppose it was justified to be guarded when you were a minor celebrity.

"Hey, I'm sorry. I don't mean to upset you. I just recognized you and it would have bothered me not to know for sure. Please, don't let me spoil your evening. Please, so sorry." I headed back to my seat and tucked one shoe behind the other as I sat down. My beer looked half empty at that point and I took a panic gulp and averted my eyes. What other reaction should I have expected?

"Hey," she said. I didn't dare look her direction. I told myself it was stupid to try and talk to an attractive news anchor in the first place. "Listen, that might have come out snotty. I'm sorry. Let me buy you a beer. You can join me if you'd like, I don't think my...uh, friend, is coming." Her eyes darted hopefully around the room as she spoke.

"You sure? I don't want to intrude."

"Really, it's fine. Please," she said.

I guess a little compassion can go a long way. I got up and took a seat at the table with her. It was then that I noticed for the first time, next to her salad bowl, a small package with a card attached to it.

"What's that?" I said.

"Oh it's nothing really, some stupid thing...for my friend."

"Oh like a present? What is it, a book or something?"

"Yeah I guess," she leaned in closer and whispered "it's seven Clark Bars."

"Seven?"

"I wish I were joking. When you say it out loud, it kind of sounds stupid doesn't it?"

"A little bit," I mused.

"It's just that he always loved them..."

"He. Hmm. Well, I know what my goal is for the evening." Sue's face turned red and she checked her phone.

"What?"

"Make enough of an impression on you to get at least eight candy bars," I said.

She let out a short burst of laughter and hit the table with her fist. I shrugged and motioned to the waitress to bring us another drink. Something told me this was where I needed to stay.

We ended up talking for the rest of the night, about wonderful, glorious, meaningless things. It started as a slow purr and rose into a crescendo of commonality. It was actually amazing the things we had in common.

We were going through the motions like two teenagers. We compared our thoughts on the best breakfast foods—French toast of course. We waxed on the demerits of slutty Halloween costumes. As the evening wore on, she started to confide in me.

"The truth is Tom, I didn't come here tonight to meet a friend."

"No?"

"Nope. I was here hoping to bump into my high school English teacher. Mr. Potter. I was so in love with him. I thought maybe there might still be something there..."

"No way."

"What?"

"You're not only really great to talk to, but you're successful and confident, and passably cute. You could get any guy you wanted, present company excluded. Why would you stalk your old English teacher?"

"Because he was an amazing mind. But...when you put it like that, it does sound a little creepy and far-fetched. I had such a wonderful connection with him! Hey? You don't think I could get you if I wanted?"

"Doubtful," I smirked, "I've got a lot going on these days. And No Shave November is coming up, so I'm going to be really busy, what with all the beard growing I plan on doing."

"Yeah, you're probably right. The English teacher is looking better and better." She leaned into me and gave me the most irresistible shoulder bump I could ever imagine. She was into me and I was into her, that much was clear. We never said anything about it, neither of us meant to fall in love in a bar. It just sort of happened.

The place was closing when we finally took a breath and forced ourselves to say goodbyes. She gave me her card and wrote her cell phone number on the back.

It did cross my mind there had to be a reason why she was still single, some big flaw that would explain why she gave me, of all people, her card. I imagined it came down to her being married to her job and didn't think much beyond it.

I had turned thirty and resigned myself to living as a bachelor for the rest of my life. And it wasn't like I didn't have my chances. I threw plenty of spaghetti up on the ceiling, but none of it had stuck.

I wasn't expecting much different from Sue at first. I might have been head over heels, but I imagined after a few dates she would grow tired of my wit and move on, if she went out with me at all. She had a lot of things going for her. She was clearly a decent person, very pretty and quasi-famous, at least in this town. I was convinced I wouldn't be much of a prize to her. The expectation was she could find a mate far superior to the senior technical architect of a software company, who lived alone and was considering getting a cat.

The aroma of our mutual interest was still wafting in the air when I called to ask her on a proper date.

"Hello?"

"Sue? This is Tom. We met the other nigh..."

"Tom, you called! Did you seriously think I wouldn't remember you? We shut down Bernie's."

"Yeah, I guess I pride myself on not being presumptuous."

"What's up Tom?"

"I'd like to see you again. Buy you food and the whole thing. If you're interested," I said.

"Yeah I think we can do that. Wha'dya have in mind?"

"Oh. Um, great. Well...well to be honest, not to sound like a complete dork-a-saur-"

"Too late."

"-I hadn't really planned anything. I figured you would be too busy being on TV and combing your hair to actually say yes. But I knew I'd kill myself if I didn't at least ask."

"Well I said yes, so pick me up at the TV station a quarter till eight Thursday and impress me. I'm glad you called and I should act way more hard to get, but I gotta get back to work. See you later?"

"Yep, yes. Thursday."

"Good talking to you Tom. See ya."

And then she hung up. She one hundred percent controlled our first phone call. I was a mouse and she was a cat batting me around, playfully. I thought of nothing but her leading up to that first date.

I picked her up exactly on time. I wore my least wrinkled button-down shirt and bought a brand new pair of jeans for the occasion. This was the big show. I was never much for impressing a girl with falsehoods, so to counteract my new pants, I decided to show her the real me.

I called it my "sweatpants date." The only true way to make sure a girl was the real deal. I wasn't about to shower Sue with a three-hundred-dollar meal or rent a limo to drive us through town. In fact, most of that stuff seemed stupid and disingenuous. I needed to take her someplace I loved and not be too over the top.

I took Sue to my favorite dumpling bar with the dingy counters, sweet ginger smell, and ripped vinyl booths.

She didn't utter a single complaint as we sat down and allowed me to order sake for us. The first words out of her mouth were, "This place smells amazing. How did you find it?"

This immediately put my nerves to bed and we had another fantastic night of conversation.

The night ended quite differently than our first encounter. After dinner, we went on a stroll through the neighborhood, holding hands. We shared a kiss under a giant martini glass hanging outside of a small club nearby. The electricity I felt could have powered a small city.

In fact, we saw each other every day for the next three months. It was the best ninety-two days of my life. On day ninety-three, Sue dropped the bomb on me. She had cardiomyopathy and was already well over what was generally the expected lifespan for the disease.

I was sitting down when she told me the first time. She said, through tears, I could walk away and never look back. I don't know which was more upsetting, learning the woman I loved was dying or the fact she could push me away so easily.

I stared at her for a while, trying to find something that would tell me she was actually sick. To me she looked normal. She was beautiful and petite, healthy, strong, smart, awkward and funny, and she was mine. I couldn't fathom not having her around.

Looking back of course there were signs. She would get exhausted much more easily than anyone else. She rarely drank more than one drink at a time, if any. She ate like a bird, though I always attributed that to her on-air look.

After it was out in the open, she was left hysterically crying. Then, as if she had dumped me or something, she began repeatedly apologizing for all the tears and trouble she was causing me. As she was blubbering on, I worried that I had already lost her.

"I've never let myself fall in love before. This is why. Someday I'll die. We won't get to choose when. And you'll be alone and it makes me sick to think about."

I held her closer than I ever had before night, calming her down before she said something she might regret.

"Sue, you've finally found me and I'm not going anywhere. I'm lucky. I get to spend the rest of your life loving you. Let me do that. Marry me."

The words spilled out of my mouth like water boiling over onto the stove. I couldn't stop it. I didn't want to. I'd fallen in love and, sick or not, Sue wasn't going to get rid of me without a fight.

"Marry me," I said more confidently as I overlooked the fact I had neither a ring or the blessing of her father, both of which I eventually got. All I could do was smile and kiss her with the mighty lips of a man that knew what he wanted.

It worked. Still crying she nodded her head and buried her face in the crook of my neck. And thus, we began the path to commitment.

In truth, I was hesitant at first. I knew I loved her, but the logistics of the whole thing made me seriously consider for the first time, that she might die and leave me.

We quickly threw together a bohemian wedding. It was spur of the moment, but it felt right. She wore off white and I wore sneakers. The ceremony was under the setting sun with a handful of friends bearing witness.

It was quick, it was amazing and there we were. We lay in our marital bed that night marveling at one another.

"Mrs. Tom Winters," I cooed.

"Mr. Sue Anderson," she retorted.

"How on earth did we get so lucky to sit next to each other at Bernie's? Fate."

"Do we believe in fate?" she said.

"I don't see why not. I'm here aren't I? You are here. What else is there?"

"Well I'm attractive and famous and you couldn't resist me. Seems like the standard fodder for a proper love story."

"Well naturally," I said. "But I still can't help but think that we have been somehow enchanted. Or at least I have."

"Well speak for yourself. I'm here through sheer effort."

"Oh?" I rolled over on my side to face her.

"I shouldn't even be alive; it is only my resolve that puts me in your bed. And not to sound too pretentious, it was all me, my own hard work. Thank God you came along. Otherwise, my life would still revolve around what I was eating or not eating, how much exercise I was getting, what combination of medicine I was taking. I was the shell of a woman trying to just keep working, not really living."

I propped myself up on my elbow and smiled at her. "Well I don't want you to stop those things. I intend to keep you around for a while."

She kissed me and leaned in closer to whisper in my ear, "be careful what you wish for."

"No really. Not only is your regiment impressive, your level of dedication is just another in a long list of reasons why I love you. Willpower is so hard to come by these days."

"Willpower? I call it stubbornness."

"Either way, I wish I could clone everything about you."

"Kids? I don't think so. It'd break my heart," she said.

Then she rolled off the bed and began messing with the thermostat on the wall. I lay there watching her naked body sway from side to side. She moved with grace and beauty, though I could tell she was uncomfortable with where the conversation had turned.

"Well, that's settled then," I said trying to remain light-hearted. She turned and shot me a glance. The type of glance you shouldn't expect to see on your wedding night. It wasn't mean or angry, it wasn't sad or pathetic. It was unexplained. Like the Mona Lisa smile. I wasn't sure what to make of it other than choosing my next words carefully.

I wasn't angry exactly, I hadn't considered having a kid either. I think at the time I was more caught off guard than anything the decision was made and put to bed without my input. Looking back, I don't fault her for feeling that way.

"Sue, you know I love you and I'll support you no matter what. Please come back to bed. I want you. No, I crave you. Let's do sexy time."

Her left eye quivered slightly and she managed a smile. "Mr. Winter, you sure know what to say to make a lady feel special. Poets will speak of your name, sexy time will be put on t-shirts and coffee mugs the world over!"

She got close enough to the side of the bed and I gently pulled her down to my level. We found our bodies moving like flour being sifted, falling together into one single entity, indistinguishable from one another. I never again brought up the notion of children and neither did she.

***

After the wedding, Sue and I moved into a townhouse in the northside of Chicago. Sue had a respectable walking commute to her TV station, and I was able to work almost exclusively from home. It worked out well.

I would make her breakfast every morning and tell her I loved her as she slipped out the door to prepare for the evening news. Nothing was hard, everything was an oil painting waiting to happen. I was never happier.

Sue had a knack of taking something as pedestrian as going to a bookstore and amplifying it into something that couldn't be forgotten for two lifetimes. It wasn't just a bookstore; it was a reading by an author I loved. It wasn't a restaurant; it was a private cooking class with the head chef.

We were out there always, never afraid to try new things and always willing to one up each other with the next big adventure or secret episode in what was our life. Bliss doesn't begin to describe it.

It wasn't all puppy dogs and ice cream though. It's true, the good times went unmatched, but we had our little things like anyone else. For me, her work schedule was often to blame for one argument or another. Of course I was being petty or selfish, but she had a very bad habit of not coming home when she said she would.

In truth, her going out wasn't what made me mad, it was when she would assure me that she would be home at a specific time and then blow past that time with little remorse. When she finally would call to apologize and tell me she was on her way, she still wouldn't come home for another couple of hours.

Sometimes after she would finally walk in the door, I would pretend to be sleep. It was my passive aggressive way of letting her know I was annoyed. Usually when I did this, she would still manage to win me over. Sometimes it was a cute note left on my forehead, sometimes she would shake me awake and beg for forgiveness.

I don't think she ever realized how much it bothered me. She was consistent and regimented in almost all facets of her life, but when it came to committing to a specific time to come home to me, she was the worst.

Most of the time I let her know I was disappointed and would roll over and go to bed. But sometimes I would waste a lot of breath trying to explain to her it wasn't about coming home late, it was about being truthful. If she wasn't planning on coming home until two in the morning, then say that.

Every once in a while, usually late at night after a long day or one of our arguments, Sue would break down. I always suspected she did this before I came along, when she was alone, but it didn't make it any less scary.

It was during one of these late night sobbing sessions she first started her living will. She would cry and pull out this elaborate folder for planning or plotting the events leading up to her death. She was determined not to be a burden.

I didn't say anything at first. I knew it was morbid and morose, but it was her choice. And it honestly didn't bother me too much. But then, it turned into an obsession. She would spend hours upon hours working out the details; every aspect of her demise. It wasn't only the will, it was the funeral home, the burial plot, the music and flowers. Whether I was going to shave or not, what suit I was going to wear, what dress she would be buried in.

It was taking over everything about her and us. Finally, I confronted her about it. She did such a good job not letting her cardiomyopathy drive her life, but this death planning was doing exactly that. I couldn't take it.

"Sue," I called from our bedroom as she sat in our home office typing away. It was early in the morning and she would need to leave for the station in an hour or so. I pressed my hand on her vacant side of the bed and it was cold. A simple indication she had been up for a while.

When she didn't answer, I pulled myself out of bed and stepped into a pair of jogging shorts. I meandered into the office.

"Sue?"

"Yes dear," she replied without looking up. She was frantically typing. She was already fully dressed and had her hair rolled up into a bun with a pencil.

"What you working on?" I tried to sound casual.

"Oh not much. Just some research."

A few books lay open next to her. One was about power of attorney and another about life insurance.

"Sue, you're spending more and more time lately planning for death. Let's cross that bridge when we come to it. It's taking away from us actually living."

She looked up at me with anger behind her bloodshot eyes. I put my hands in front of her as a peace offering.

"Tom, this isn't an argument you want to start. You can't win."

"You're doing everything right. You eat well, exercise, go to the doctor regularly. Your symptoms are completely managed by medicine and lifestyle changes. You are solid as a rock. Don't overlook everything you have worked on to be the person you are today. I'm not trying to argue, I'm just worried about you."

"Well don't. I've waited long enough, I have to do this stuff now, for your sake. I will not be a burden on you or my family. Besides, this is like the fourth or fifth version. I have already had a few notarized."

I shook my head and sighed. I wanted to tell her she was merely feeling sorry for herself and she would never be a burden, but I didn't. Even in my head, it sounded too harsh. Instead, I opted to not say anything. I smiled and moved to pat her on the back.

When I got to the other side of the desk, Sue looked at me with glossy eyes. "Tom, I have to do this. I'm not going to leave this stuff to you."

"Sweetheart, you aren't going anywhere. Don't worry about this stuff. Enjoy what we have now. There will be plenty of time for that later."

"How can you say that?" She stood up, the chair wheeled itself hard into the bookshelf behind her, "I'm on borrowed time already. Oh God." Sue started to desert me and leave the room in a huff, but I caught her in my arms and pulled her close to me.

"Calm down. I'm just asking you to be present is all. I love you and it's hard to watch you spend all your time planning your demise. It's not healthy."

She struggled a bit, trying to wiggle free from my grasp. "Well, it's a good thing I'm already sick. Tom, please. I want to be alone right now. I love you too, but I don't want to talk about it."

Finally pulling herself free from my grip, she started out of the room. Then she stopped herself, turned and looked at me for a moment. Then she wiped the tears that had started to roll down her cheek with the sleeve of her blouse. She crossed the room and kissed me on the cheek before turning and hurriedly ran out of the room.

***

I waited ten minutes before I called her on the phone. I figured I would tell her I was sorry for pressing her and that I wanted her to be happy. She didn't answer on the first try. I immediately called back and she answered.

"Hello?"

"Hey, I wanted to let you know that I love you and I'm sorry I got you all worked up."

There was silence on the other end of the line for a moment. I could hear the sounds of the city around her as she walked down the sidewalk. "Thank you," she said.

"Can I make it up to you, my love?" I said.

I listened to her breathing for a moment, trying to subtly match her cadence. "What did you have in mind?"

"Delta Spirit is playing at the Paradise tonight. Maybe we could check it out. It's a late show, so we shouldn't miss much."

"Yeah sure..." her voice trailed off in the middle of her thought. I sat on the other end of the line wondering what had caught her attention.

"OH MY GOD!" She screamed half into her cell phone and half out into the street. Later I would learn that she slipped her phone into her jacket pocket at this point. I stayed on the line and heard everything that transpired.

At first it was merely the sounds of fabric scraping against the phone on the inside of her pocket, it was rushed and sounded a lot like objects knocking into each other when you are searching through a junk drawer for something meaningful.

I tried to get her attention. "Sue? Sue? Are you there?" She hadn't hung up the phone and a few seconds later I heard her again.

"Stop! Please."

Again I heard the sound of rubbing fabric. She was running at that point. Towards a nowhere man. Witnesses on the scene reported he was drunk, physically standing, but mentally passed out and standing in the middle of the street. It was mid-morning and the weather was overcast. To be drunk on a Wednesday morning meant he was quite indifferent with having his life saved as the garbage truck barreled towards him.

From the details in the police report, Sue wasted no time charging towards the man. She tugged at his jacket repeatedly and tried to coax him out of the road by taking his bag in her hands.

"You can't be here. It's not safe," she said.

These would end up being her last words.

She pushed the man towards the sidewalk and the rusted red garbage truck struck her with full force at 8:18 a.m. Eastern Time. The sound of the impact reverberated through the phone and eventually settled into the inside of my ears. It took me hours to understand the gravity of that moment. I'm not sure I even understand it now.

Suzanne Elaine Anderson Winter died instantly. There was no saying goodbye. Her heart held up its end of the bargain as long as it could. This was the ultimate curveball and she never saw it coming. Her body was thrown fifteen feet backwards and landed mercilessly onto the street.

When the sound coming through the phone stopped, I began calling her name. First as a whisper, then louder and louder. I could still hear the rumble of the truck's diesel engine and a few sporadic voices shouting, though muffled through her jacket pocket.

I continued to press the phone to my ear, harder than necessary. I covered my other ear with my hand attempting to hear what was going on. As I did this, I threw on some pants and headed outside. I turned and began down the sidewalk in front of our house. We had moved to the city so we could abandon the need for cars. I was barefoot and proceeded to move through the route that would have taken Sue towards the TV station.

My mouth hung wide open the entire time. I moved with fervor and earnest. At this point, I wasn't sure yet what I would find when I reached her. She would be hurt, but to what extent my brain couldn't comprehend. She was dead, but it would take hours before I would relay those words to myself and agree to that reality.

The love of my life was still lying in the street when I turned the corner and spotted the gathering crowd. The rest of the day was all sorts of wrong. Blood on my shirt, riding with her body to the hospital. Guilt for singing along to a Pearl Jam song I overheard as I escorted her limp and cold body into the hospital. The small room with lots of doctors and nurses talking towards me and receiving nothing in return but blank stares and wet cheeks.

Somehow that day, I managed to call her father. I punished him with sobbing and enough details to bring him on his way. "It was an accident," I told him. Later we would hug and mutually agree her heart was strong right up until the end. Life wasn't fair. She was tough and brave and life wasn't fair.

Later, thanks to Don, her mother and sister received the news and joined us. The family held each other tight and hummed softly to avoid more tears. For a few fleeting moments, I felt like an outsider. I smiled politely, leaning against a wall to keep myself from collapsing.

I remember never making it to bed that night. I sat in the waiting room of the hospital, waiting for nothing. But I had nowhere else to go. I was cold and alone with no more tears left. To say I was lost was an understatement.

In the morning I came home to our empty house, broken. In the office on the desk was Sue's death plan. As I stood and stared at the neat mess of paperwork, I fell into a trance, muttering to myself over and over, "What am I going to do? What am I going to do?"

CHAPTER TWELVE
Ann 2011

I sat on the back of my calves like a baseball player waiting to catch the ball. Mascara was running down my tear soaked face and I was picking a piece of tobacco off of my tongue as I twisted a lit cigarette in my other hand.

I remember my overcoat scraping against the pavement next to the trashcan I was hiding behind. I was an ugly crier and I didn't want anyone to see the mother of all sob sessions. My best friend, Sue, was two weeks removed from being killed and I wasn't handling it very well.

When I first heard the news, I couldn't believe it. I'd been preparing myself for a phone call like it for years, but I always thought it would be her heart, not something as pointless as getting hit by a garbage truck.

It was almost too cliché to even picture in my head. But, regardless of how morbid it truly was, I did picture that truck making impact with my poor darling Sue, over and over. Sometimes I did it to remember how pretty she was. Other times, it bubbled to the surface somewhere in the middle of my marathon of tears.

I stayed behind the trashcan for a few more minutes, waiting for peace that would never come. Eventually I would have to go inside. When I did finally stand up and wipe my face with my palms, the only person I could see was Tom.

He had his back to me and he was talking to someone outside of my line of sight. The other person was standing around the corner of the house, somewhere on the walkway leading to the front step.

Tom looked utterly lost in the moment. I lingered a moment watching him. He swayed back and forth, almost as if someone else was controlling him.

I leaned on the trashcan and it moved, causing a scraping sound across the driveway. He turned, facing my direction, towards the driveway and the street. He must have been past the uncontrollable crying phase, though his face was flush with the mid-morning sun. I shook my shoulders inside of my jacket and stepped out from behind the trashcan.

When I approached Tom, he jumped slightly. I could see his shoulders tense up. He might have been expecting another awkwardly consoling moment, like the ones I got from both of Sue's parents. When he saw it was me, he issued the standard, I'm holding it together smile.

"Ann. I'm glad you're here," he said.

"Hey Tom. Is everyone already inside?" I didn't quite have the guts to look him in the eyes, so I spoke to his chin. Tom and I had only met briefly once or twice in the short lifespan of his marriage to my best friend. We weren't quite past the nervous phase, but in that moment I was probably the closest person he had to family around.

"Yeah, almost everyone." He let the words hang in the air. "We probably shouldn't keep them waiting." Half-heartedly, he pointed towards the front door. Sue had only been in the ground a short time and I don't think Tom knew what he was going to do from there.

Standing outside of Don's house was ominous and almost felt like the final step in accepting she was really gone. After this formality was over, what was left? I suppose we would continue grieving, each in our own way. My way was going to be to gain ten pounds on eating ice cream and drinking bourbon.

I took his arm gingerly, "You think you're going to make it?" We made eye contact for the first time. My face was still damp from my tears. The color of my cheeks echoed his and I squeezed his arm a little tighter, "Come on, let's go."

He didn't say anything, but he allowed me to guide him to the porch. As we entered the house, he immediately let out a deep sigh.

"Ann, this whole thing is so messed...I don't want to ever have to go through this again," he said.

I nodded in agreement and we wandered through the entryway looking for signs of life among the silence of the big house. We were there for the official reading of Sue's will. This was really happening.

I wasn't sure who would show up given that Sue didn't have a fortune to dole out and had never even mentioned a will to me. I expected a small gathering.

As we entered the living room, I saw Catherine and Ethan standing inside the kitchen having a conversation. I started in their direction and expected Tom to do the same. When he didn't budge I decided to stay with him, in case he was about to go into total meltdown. In truth, I was barely holding on, but being there by his side gave me a purpose and helped to keep me together.

"I know it's hard, Tom, but it's almost over. Stick with me," I said. I could taste the whiskey I had dumped down my throat in my car before I ducked behind the trash bins to cry.

The sun poured through the creases of the curtains and bounced off everything within its reach. It seemed to lighten the mood and soon Tom worked up his bravest smile while the rest of the party made their way into the living room.

A man, who introduced himself as Jack, approached with Sue's Mom close behind.

"Thank you for coming today. Sue wanted you to be here and I'm glad you made it," Tom said.

It was a canned answer for sure, but Tom's voice wore it with a state of sincerity and it instantly broke down weird feelings. Jack nodded as Jackie pulled Tom in for a hug. He received it warmly, closing his eyes as she squeezed.

The room had been set up with a makeshift podium made out of a small card table and some old medical books. Surrounding the books were these neat little brown packages and envelopes. Each perfectly wrapped in packing paper, nine in total. There was also a tenth package, leaning against the wall behind the table.

The packages were endearing to me in a way. It was like Sue to have something so elegant planned for her last occasion.

As Tom and I took a seat on a small loveseat near the podium, the room felt warm and inviting. The fireplace had been lit and the couch next to us seemed to hold more pillows than necessary.

Jackie moved from one person to another, carefully socializing with each attendee. She was beautiful in a shiny black dress and her hair was folded into a neat pile on her head. She had evidently run out of tears as well, but her puffy cheeks put her in the same club as Tom and I. She felt right at home in the house. She had turned it back over to Don after the divorce was finalized.

I motioned for her to sit near us and she politely waved me off. As she did, Don emerged from the kitchen with his new girlfriend, Katerina. She was slender and wore a pale green shawl over a muted black dress. Neither spoke as they took a seat on the couch centered in the room.

They were immediately followed by a stout man in a deep blue suit. He carried a manila folder and cleared his throat as he took his place behind the podium. Catherine and Ethan soon took seats as well. I tried to make eye contact with Catherine, but eventually gave up as she seemed content to give Ethan her attention.

Sue's sister, Sam, finally appeared. She came out of the kitchen followed by a group of men. The first was Charlie, Sue's college boyfriend. I hadn't seen him in years, but we exchanged a knowing glance as he sat down across the room. Next came Dr. Norris, Sue's doctor. He checked his watch a few times before crossing the room and settling onto the couch next to Katerina.

The last man, dressed in a beige sports jacket and jeans didn't take a seat. He stood in the shadows by the fireplace alternating different ways to cross his arms in an effort to appear comfortable. I leaned towards Don. "Is that Mr. Potter?" He merely nodded, but remained silent.

When everyone was seated, the dapper man behind the podium opened the folder and cleared his throat. "This afternoon we are gathered to read the last will and testament of one, Suzanne Elaine Anderson Winter." He looked at Tom as he spoke and gave a slight nod. "My name is Archibald Wentz, attorney to Mr. Anderson. I have been given the difficult task of reading Sue's will. After the reading, Don would welcome you to stay and remember Sue's life over drinks here in the den."

He paused, cleared his throat and motioned to Tom. "Before we begin, Mr. Winter would like to say a few words." And with that Mr. Wentz side-stepped away from the podium and Tom rose and zigzagged his way to the front of the room. I watched his hands. They were struggling to find somewhere to go. Eventually they settled onto the corners of the books that sat on top of the card table.

Tom stood there, his eyes fixated on the fire burning in the fireplace beyond the gathering of people. Before the silence became deafening, moments before I was about to jump up and pull him back to the safety of his seat, he spoke.

"For those of you that don't know me, my name is Tom. I, I just wanted to say a few words before the will was read. After the..."

He choked on his words. The lawyer moved to Tom's side and offered him a tissue, which he accepted and wadded up in his hands. He continued, "After the accident I...Sue had been planning this day for a while. She spent a significant amount of her spare time working on her will and making sure her affairs were in order, as I'm sure her parents can attest to. She had her funeral and burial completely arranged and paid for years ago. She also had book after book about death and grieving, waiting for me when this time came. She was determined not to leave me holding the bill and wanted me...and all of you to be at peace."

His eyes wandered the room. Sam tucked her hands under her armpits and looked up at the ceiling, trying not to cry. I made eye contact with Catherine. I thought back to the night we made-out. We had bonded, not just by kissing, but also through the all the worry that came with being with Sue in the hospital shortly before she moved back home. My eyes started to water and I broke our gaze.

"Before we read the will," Tom said, "it was Sue's wish that everyone in attendance today find the time to reflect and make peace with Sue's passing through story telling. She wanted it to be like Thanksgiving, only instead of gathering around a dead turkey, it would be her. She...made me say that."

He smiled awkwardly and stepped out from behind the table. When he came back to join me on the love seat for the reading of the will, he sat a little closer. His knee was bouncing frantically as Mr. Wentz prepared to read Sue's simple yet generous will to the group.

Mr. Wentz pushed on a pair of reading glasses, cleared his throat and began:

Ever since I found out I had a fading heart my life became structured. I went to great lengths to stay alive, though at first I wasn't sure why. As a result, part of me was lost in the process. I chose what I ate very carefully. I exercised to ensure I had a balanced metabolism. I turned going to the doctor's office into a sacrament. It took time, but I was able to find the right level of medicine and lifestyle changes to make things seem almost normal, most days.

Life became a series of adjustments, an inch this way, an inch that way. All to make sure I would be around long enough to fulfill my dreams. But somewhere along the way I lost sight of what truly makes a person happy.

Yes, I graduated college and lived all over the country. Yes, I fulfilled my dream of doing the news on camera. I even went on the trip of a lifetime with my father to Africa. I was never hungry, never poor, never out on the street. But I did live in a prison of my own design, one that kept true joy at bay in an effort to prolong the inevitable.

That being said, I'm trying to throw aside the structure that has been holding me down and make changes in my life. My loving and wonderful husband Tom has helped me realize that love is worth more. So here I am writing my will, not with some pre-formatted template, but with my heart. It's all I ever wanted and what's a summary of your entire life without a little emotion and feeling?

So without further ado, I, Suzanne Elaine Anderson Winter, being of sound mind and hanging onto the slight semblance of an ordinary state of health, make my last will and testament in a manner that follows. I will try to keep this brief; you have no idea at the amount of edits I had to make to get it to where we are now. Consider yourself lucky you made the role sheet.

To my darling husband, Thomas Henry Winter, who has already given me so much, to him I leave my all my personal possessions which are herein not ex-

plicitly mentioned. Everything from my clothes to the ugly moon shaped plate I painted at the pottery place on our third date. I know he will keep the things that are truly dear to him and then pass the rest of my belongings to my family and friends who would love to do the same. I'll never stop loving you, Tom.

I give to my dear father, Donald Fredrick Anderson, who I can only imagine is putting on a brave face for you today, my Makonde African wood carvings and my regional Emmys. Both are dear to me and I would love for you to take care of them.

To my Mother, Jackie Alice Anderson, I leave my diplomas, my childhood photo album and my diamond solitaire earrings. I know it isn't much considering you brought me into the world, but I love you none-the-less. Also take my red wool sweater. I know you hated that thing, maybe now it can bring you joy.

To my sister, Samantha Evelyn Anderson, I leave my complete 401k balance, a little over $27,000. I know you'll use it wisely and without caution. Please buy a lot of gummy bears little sis.

To Ann Maureen Caldwell, I leave my frequent flyer mileage. You always encouraged me to live and explore and to be myself. Never stop moving on my account. Thank you for everything and then some.

To Charlie Thomas Finch, I have packaged up our annoying love letters and photos from college. I would like you to have them to remind you of all of the times I foolishly pushed you away.

To Jack Emerson Rogers, I leave my vintage VHS copy of the Lion King. Do good things.

To Ethan Matthew Hammond, I leave my copy of Wildflowers by Tom Petty. Listen to it under the stars.

To Dr. Ralph T. Norris, I have arranged, at Sullivan's diner on 33rd Street, to buy you breakfast for every year that I lived. I have you to thank for the last decade and I hope you accept this tiny gesture.

To Catherine Renee Fields, I leave you my Caravaggio print. I know you'll keep it safe. Keep being yourself and you'll never lose.

To Kevin Jasper Potter, the man who defined me as a student and a leader among my peers, what can I possibly leave you worth the time you gave me? Please accept a small token of my appreciation by accepting this package of seven Clark Bars.

As he read each section of the will, he would pause and hold up one of the neat brown packages from the table. These evidently were the gifts Sue had left for everyone. Mine was a simple envelope I assumed contained information about the frequent flyer miles Sue had left. When he was finished reading, two envelopes remained. Mr. Wentz then paused and scanned the room. Halfway through this strange pass he pulled off his reading glasses. Then he said, "It seems there are a few folks named in the will not present. I will read the portion of the will that pertains to them for recording purposes and will do my due diligence to find these individuals and deliver their belongings."

To Daniel Collins, who knew me at a strange time, yet left a lasting impression on me, I leave my well-worn vintage hardback copy of Jane Austen's Pride and Prejudice. I hope it keeps you warm at night.

To Josie Penner, I leave the balance of $255 plus another $25 for a tip for services not yet rendered. This should settle our affairs. Thank you for your kindness.

And that's all. I hope I've left each of you with a small sense of love and importance as you go through this tough time. I never expected to be here longer than I was allowed and I cherished each and every one of you and the time we shared. Be good to each other and I wish you health and happiness for the rest of your days.

Yours truly,
Sue Anderson

When he was finished saying her name, no one moved a muscle. The silence lasted at least a minute as everyone collectively stared into the fire, reflecting on the loss of Sue.

Finally, Don stood up. "We have drinks in the kitchen. I invite all of you to stay for as long as you like. The family and I have prepared a meal for those that stick around."

It took everyone a few drinks and a plate of Don's famous barbecue wings to loosen up. Eventually, we started playing songs that reminded us of Sue, telling old stories and laughing at stupid things we did with Sue in high school.

I hung close to Tom most of the evening. He still seemed stiff and awkward around the rest of the group. Eventually he grew comfortable enough to laugh and marvel at some of the stories we told about Sue.

Dr. Norris took his leave after a single brandy and just as it looked like the evening was coming to an end, Mr. Potter approached Tom and I.

"Ann. It's so strange seeing you without Rachel and Sue glued to your side." His voice trembled as he spoke.

"Mr. Potter, I wasn't even sure if you were still alive," I said. "I've been working up the nerve to come talk to you."

He looked perplexed, "Why wouldn't I be alive? I'm only forty-two. Jesus, you must have thought I was ancient in high school!"

Tom chuckled. "I don't think we've been properly introduced. I'm Sue's...well, I *was* Sue's husband."

Mr. Potter held out his hand to shake Tom's. "Don't sell yourself short. You are and always will be her husband. Don't take that away from yourself. She was an amazing young lady, you're lucky to have crossed paths with her."

Tom's face turned a shade of red and he disappeared momentarily into his glass of wine. When he finished his long drink he cleared his throat and said, "Seven Clark Bars, huh?"

Mr. Potter shifted in his shoes and grabbed my shoulder for stability. He was looking at the ground. "Ha, well I always did love those things. Sue and

Ann here would bring them to me in class sometimes. Brown-nosers." He smiled and pushed his hands into his pockets.

"We just wanted to get out of doing homework. I don't think it ever worked though!" I said trying to think back at a time when Mr. Potter actually did assign homework.

"Well, Sue must have liked you an awful lot to bring you all the way over here for a box of candy," Tom said.

"I guess so. I wanted to pay my respects. She was something special and I'm sorry she's gone. I had no idea at all she was in poor health," Mr. Potter said.

"So you didn't keep up with her after high school?" Tom asked.

"Well I would have, but you know how things go. We get busy. Even still, I could tell a story or two about her from back then. And this one here too!" He put his arm around me and I went a little stiff. I thought better of outright rejecting him and simply smiled.

"Sue wanted us to tell stories. That's a great idea, Mr. Potter."

"Please, call me Kevin."

"Kevin, please indulge us with a story." Tom said with fire in his eyes.

I wasn't sure why Tom was so interested in hearing what Mr. Potter had to say, but eventually he urged everyone in the room to refill their drinks and to settle into a seat. He goaded and goaded Mr. Potter until, resigned he took his place at the front of the room.

"Well, I supposed I can find a story to share about Sue for such a captive audience. All I ask in return is for someone else to do the same. To Tom's point earlier, it was what she would have wanted. This should be a night to celebrate all Sue was and will be. A few well-told stories would certainly do her the honor she deserves."

Don stoked the fire and dimmed the lights slightly. Tom and I once again sat on the love seat, and this time I intentionally sat as close to him as I could.

I knew Sue had a thing for Mr. Potter at one point. I wasn't sure what his story was going to be about and I couldn't guarantee it wouldn't be upsetting for Tom. Having him close to me was insurance.

I looked around the room. Jack and Jackie were picking at a veggie tray on a table between them. Ethan and Sam were snuggled up on the couch, each under a pillow eager to hear a story. Don and Katerina, who had been slowly meandering around the room picking up plates and empty cups, had settled down onto the edge of the fireplace arm in arm. They too were anxious to hear a story. Catherine sat alone and Charlie was pulling on his coat in the corner, attempting to inch out.

"Charlie!" I yelled. "Stick around a while longer; I want to catch up."

I wasn't sure in the moment if I meant it or not, but something in me wanted everyone to hear what Mr. Potter had to say. I still respected him as a teacher and wanted everyone else to follow suit.

We all turned our attention back to Mr. Potter. He had removed his sports jacket and draped it effortlessly across the table that once held all those clean blank looking packages. Sue must have spent a lot of time folding and creasing the paper to give them that look of perfection.

As I thought about the packages and my own personal bequeathing, Mr. Potter began.

"It was all pageantry, as it should have been. It was a high school graduation, after all..."

Whether you enjoyed Twelve and a Half Hearts or not, please consider leaving a review. This helps other readers decide on the difficult decision to choose this book!

If you would like to be notified when Ian Cahill releases new books, check out iancahill.com and sign up for the mailing list.

You can also connect with Ian on Twitter and Instagram @iancahill for more great content.